I0609987

James Brown Scouller

History of the Big Spring Presbytery of the United
Presbyterian Church

and its territorial predecessors, 1750-1879

James Brown Scouller

History of the Big Spring Presbytery of the United Presbyterian Church
and its territorial predecessors, 1750-1879

ISBN/EAN: 9783337367909

Printed in Europe, USA, Canada, Australia, Japan

Cover: Foto ©Andreas Hilbeck / pixelio.de

More available books at **www.hansebooks.com**

OF THE

BIG SPRING PRESBYTERY

OF THE

UNITED PRESBYTERIAN CHURCH,

AND

ITS TERRITORIAL PREDECESSORS,

1750-1879.

PREFACE.

THE Presbytery of Big Spring at its meeting in Mexico, October 1, 1878, passed the following resolution :—

Resolved, That the Presbytery of Big Spring do hereby request the Rev. J. B. Scouller to prepare a history of this Presbytery, and in case of his undertaking the work, the sketches of congregations shall be forwarded to him.

In accordance with this request, an attempt has been made to narrate briefly, not merely the history of the Presbytery of Big Spring, but of all the churches, whether Reformed Presbyterian, or Associate, or Associate Reformed, or United Presbyterian, which have existed or do still exist within the territorial bounds of this Presbytery; for they have been so intimately related to each other that their histories cannot well be separated. The minutes of the Presbyteries which covered this ground from 1782 to 1803, are lost, and the subsequent ones are more or less imperfect. A few congregations kept records, but the most of them did not until very recently; and some of the congregations dissolved so long ago that few if any are old enough to remember them. All records, and documents, and memoirs, and family papers, and family traditions which could be found, bearing upon the history of Scottish Presbyterianism between the Susquehanna river and the Allegheny mountain, have been carefully examined, and imperfect and unsatisfactory as the following history may be in some parts, it is still a consolation to believe that it is more full and complete than could have been written at any subsequent period, for the sources of information are every year becoming less.

J. B. S.

NEWVILLE, PA.

History of the Presbytery of Big Spring.

CHAPTER I.

THE PLANTING--FROM 1730 TO 1782.

THE Presbytery of Big Spring did not exist in form and name until 1803, yet many of its churches are of older date, and some of them were among the first of the denomination. In 1730 the first white settler crossed the Susquehanna river to make his home and to build his fortune in the Kittatinny Valley, the valley of the Blue Mountain, as that wide and fertile valley was then called by the Indians, which extends from the Susquehanna to the Potomac. When this barrier was once passed, so great became the tide of immigration, that within six years, a chain of settlements stretched from river to river, and in 1751 the white inhabitants in what is now Cumberland and Franklin counties amounted to about five thousand persons. Of these not over fifty families were German, who had located in the edge of Franklin. The others were all from the British Isles, and at least two-thirds of them were from the north of Ireland. A variety of causes ministered to the rapid settlement of this section of country by the Irish. The land was fertile and well watered; it was level and inviting; the bounding mountains lay far apart, removing all fear or sense of crowding, and the acreage of its area exceeded that of their own county of Antrim. Constitutionally brave and fond of adventure, they had no fear of Indians or wild beasts, and went readily to the frontier. The Irish did not begin to emigrate to Pennsylvania till 1719, but from some causes, which

6

cannot here be well explained,* they then commenced to pour in
in such numbers that Secretary Logan wrote in 1729: "It looks
as if Ireland is to send all her inhabitants hither, for last week
not less than six ships arrived, and every day two or three ar-
rive also. The common fear is that if they continue to come
they will make themselves the proprietors of the province. It
is strange that they thus crowd where they are not wanted.
The Indians themselves are alarmed at the swarms of strangers,
and we are afraid of a breach between them, for the Irish are
very rough to them." They located mainly in the vicinity of
the Susquehanna river. In Lancaster and Dauphin counties,
settlements were first made along the Octorara, the Pequea, the
Conestoga, the Swatara and the other smaller streams which
empty into the Susquehanna from the east. In habits and disposition they were convivial, quick-tempered and belligerent,
and soon became a great annoyance to their peaceable, phleg-
matic and non-resisting German and Quaker neighbors. Secretary Logan wrote thus of them in 1730: "I must own, from
my own experience in the Land Office, that the settlement of
five families from Ireland gives me more trouble than fifty of
any other people." In sobriety of life and gentleness of manners, they did not improve with time and an increase of numbers, but rather presumed upon their numerical strength until
even the Quaker forbearance of the Proprietaries finally became exhausted; so that in or about 1750, the year in which
Cumberland county was organized, positive orders were issued
to all the agents to sell no more land in either York or Lancaster county to the Irish; and to make very advantageous offers
to those of them who would remove from these counties to the
North Valley. These offers were so liberal that large numbers
accepted, and built their huts among the wigwams of the native inhabitants, whom they found to be peaceful, but by no
means non-resistant. New immigrants were also hurried on to

* "The rise of rents and tithes, with several bad harvests (1724–1728),
and especially the oppressions of the Government, led many to emigrate to
America, to which they were solicited by agents from the colonies. Four
thousand two hundred sailed in three years, some selling themselves for four
years to pay their passage."—History of the Presbyterian Church in Ireland, by Alexander, page 316.

the same valley, so that the population west of the Susquehanna grew very rapidly. The same causes produced substantially the same results in the smaller valleys on the north
and northwest, and along the water courses of York and
Adams counties.

The great mass of the Irish that settled west of the Susquehanna, between 1730 and 1750, had been reared in connection
with the Synod of Ulster. This must have been so, for the
Covenanters were not numerous in Ireland, and the Secession
churches were at this date just being planted there. Knowing
nothing about Dissent, or National Covenants, these immigrants brought no prejudice or bias which could prevent their
falling in harmoniously with the Presbyterian Church already
organized here. Indeed the first Irish settlers brought the
Presbyterian Church with them, for it was the seed which they
sowed that produced that great Church in this country. But
there were clusters of a few families in different localities,
which had been trained in the faith and practices of the Covenanters. These could not, and did not fraternize with the
Presbyterianism around them. They met together upon the
Sabbath, in each others' houses, for social worship, and waited
the time when an ordained ministry should bring to them the
preached word and the sealing ordinances. The Rev. Alexander Craighead, of the Presbyterian Church, strongly sympathized with them in their distinctive privileges, and preached
frequently for those of them that resided in Lancaster county,
and most probably, occasionally, for those west of the river.
Their hopes and desires were finally fully gratified in the
arrival of the Rev. John Cuthbertson from Ireland, although
a Scotchman by birth and training and Presbyterial connection. He landed at New Castle, Delaware, on the 5th of
August, 1751, and immediately commenced an exploration of
his missionary field. After preaching in Chester county,
and at Octorara, and Pequea, and Paxtang, he preached his
first sermon, in the bounds of this Presbytery, on Wednesday,
the 21st of August, at Walter Buchanan's, near the present
New Kingston, midway between Carlisle and the river. His
text was, Proverbs 8:4, "Unto you, O men, I call; and my

voice is to the sons of men." He also baptised Joseph Glen-
denning, John M'Clelland and Jane Swansie, infant children of
residents of that neighborhood. The afternoon of the same
day, he rode twenty miles to the house of Andrew Ralston,
near the Big Spring, and on the following morning preached
from Matthew 17:4, "Lord it is good for us to be here." Immediately after services, he started for the house of James Mitchell,
twenty-two miles distant, between Chambersburg and Rocky
Spring. Here he remained over the Sabbath, and preached
twice that day, and baptised a number of children. On Monday
he rode twenty miles to the house of Joseph Cochran, in the
Cove, and on Wednesday preached, and baptised some more
children. During the remainder of the week, he traveled
eastward to the house of David Dinwiddie, on Marsh creek,
Adams county. Spent the Sabbath as usual in preaching and
baptizing, and on the morrow, started on his return by the
way of York, to his headquarters, on the Octorara, in Lancaster county. After spending a month on a missionary tour to
the east, as far as Easton on the Delaware, he commenced a
second exploration through the counties of Cumberland, Franklin, Fulton, Adams and York, varying his course a little, and
going as far west as Licking creek, in Fulton county. This
circuit he made more or less frequently for twenty years. Of
the families thus visited, some were Scotch, but the greater
part, perhaps three-fourths, were Irish; and with many of
them, he was most probably previously acquainted. At this
time, there were only a few congregations of Covenanters in
Ireland, and they were so feeble as to be without pastors, and
for the preached word and ordinances, were wholly dependent
upon the occasional visit of a Scotch minister. Several years
before coming to this country, Mr. Cuthbertson went over
from Scotland to Ireland, and spent his time in circulating
among the little societies there as he was now doing here, and
thus became well acquainted with all of his faith. Some emigrated during that time, so that he met them here as old ac-
quaintances. There were now fully half as many Sons of the
Covenant in this country as were left in Ireland, so that go
where he would among them, he was meeting old friends, or

the relatives of those whom he left on the other side of the sea. He was thus specially fitted to be the apostle of Reformed Presbyterianism in the new world.

At some of Mr. Cuthbertson's preaching stations there was no meeting house for years, and at others as Carlisle, Big Spring, &c., they never arrived at that attainment. When the weather allowed, they met in their "tent," and when it was not propitious, they did the best they could in their cabins. This "tent" was pitched in a shady grove, and consisted simply in an elevated platform for the minister, where he could be seen and heard by all; a board nailed against a tree to support the Bible; a few rude benches for seats; and some boards overhead to protect the speaker from sun and rain; sometimes this shelter was extended so as to shield a part of the congregation. Thus accommodated they worshiped for hours at a time, and their communion services sometimes lasted for nine hours.

On the 23d of August, 1752, Mr. Cuthbertson held his first communion in America. It was at Stony Ridge or the Walter Buchanan or Junkin "tent," in Cumberland county. A preparatory fast day was observed; tokens of admission were dispensed; the services on the Sabbath commenced early and continued for nine hours. Mr. Cuthbertson paraphrased the 15th Psalm, and preached from John 3:35, "The father loveth the son, and hath given all things into his hand." After the sermon he prayed and sung, expounded the ordinance, debarred from and invited to the tables. The communicants came to the table singing the 24th Psalm. After the four table services were concluded, the minister exhorted the communicants, prayed and sung. After an interval of half an hour, he preached again from John 16:31, "Jesus answered them, Do ye now believe." On Monday he preached from Eph. 5:15, "See that ye walk circumspectly, not as fools, but as wise." About two hundred and fifty persons communed, and this comprised very nearly the entire number of Covenanters in this country, for the place was central, the season pleasant, and they gathered in from their different settlements in what is now the counties of Lancaster, York, Dauphin, Cumberland, Adams, Franklin and Fulton. This was the first time that the followers of Cameron

the new world. In 1661, at the re-establishment of Episco-
pacy in Ireland, the newly appointed bishops, with Jeremy Tay-
lor as their leader, turned all the Presbyterian ministers out of
their charges, upon the ground that they had never been ordained. This ignoring of Presbyterian ordination carried with
it a denial of the validity of any official act performed by a
Presbyterian minister. This was a great grievance, for it denied the validity of all Presbyterian marriages, and brought
confusion and distress into families in the matters of legiti-
macy and inheritance; and yet, in spite of every effort and remonstrance, things remained thus till 1782, when marriages
solemnized by dissenting ministers were declared valid, provided both parties belonged to the minister's church. In 1704
the Sacramental Test act was passed, which required "all persons holding any office, civil or military, or receiving any pay
or salary from the crown, or having command or place of trust
from the sovereign," to take the sacrament in the Established
Church within three months after their appointment.

This, of course, excluded all Presbyterians from civil and
military offices of every kind. From time immemorial, the
legal form of taking an oath required the individual to kiss
the Bible. This, the Seceders would not do; so they were not
permitted to take an oath under any circumstances. And when
in 1782, an act was passed to allow them to swear with the uplifted
hand, it was specially provided that they should *not* be qualified
or admitted to give evidence in any criminal cause, or serve on
juries, or hold any office or employment of trust under the
Crown. When we add to such grievances and outrages as
these the fact that there were several bad harvests between
1750 and 1760, which produced actual famine in some districts,
is it any wonder that so many of these poor Seceders tried to
get to America? The only wonder is, that any of them would
consent to remain in Ireland.

. As early as 1736, some settlers in Chester county applied to
the Associate Presbytery of Scotland for a supply of preaching.
Other applications were made from time to time by different
parties, but the Synod was so pressed to supply the home demand, that nothing was done till 1751, when James Hume and

John Jamison were appointed as missionaries to America. They both failed to fulfill their appointment; so in August, 1752, Alexander Gellatly and Andrew Bunyan were ordained to this work. But Mr. Bunyan's heart failed him, and the Rev. Andrew Arnott, of Midholm, consented to accompany Mr. Gellatly, with the privilege of returning at the end of a year. They sailed in the early summer of 1753, and upon landing, passed immediately to the eastern slope of the valley of the Susquehanna, and there, in November of the same year, they constituted themselves into the Associate Presbytery of Pennsylvania, subordinate to the Anti-Burgher Synod of Scotland. They were at once invited by the Presbytery of Newcastle, of the Synod of Philadelphia, to cast in their lot with them. This was declined, and that Presbytery forthwith issued a warning to their churches against these men as schismatics and separatists, and as being heretical on the gospel offer, the nature of faith, &c. Mr. Gellatly answered in a work of 240 pages. Messrs. Finley and Smith, of the Newcastle Presbytery, replied and Mr. Gellatly followed with another answer of 203 pages. This unexpected controversy ended favorably to the Seceders, for it brought them prominently before the public.

Mr. Gellatly settled at Octorara and Oxford, and Mr. Arnott returned home in the Summer of 1754; his place, however, was immediately supplied by James Proudfoot (now Proudfit), who continued to travel for four years among the young churches, before he settled at Pequea.

In 1758, Matthew Henderson came and settled at Oxford and Pencader. In 1761, Mr. Gellatly died, and John Mason and two probationers, Robert Annan and John Smart, arrived. Mr. Mason settled in New York city, Mr. Smart returned home, and Mr. Annan settled at Marsh creek. In 1762, William Marshall came and was soon ordained and installed at Deep Run and Neshaminy, in Bucks county.

Up till 1764 all the Associate ministers sent out from the mother country were from the Anti-Burgher Synod of Scotland; but during that year Rev. Thomas Clarke arrived from the Burgher Presbytery in Ireland, which was subordinate to the Burgher Synod of Scotland. Mr. Clarke did not wish to continue a division which could have no grounds or significancy in this country, and applied at once to the Associate Presbytery of Pennsylvania for admission. After some delay and considerable negotiation as to terms, he was admitted September 2, 1765, upon the following conditions, viz:

1. That Mr. Clarke shall not, either publicly or privately, justify the Burgess Oath, or any writing published in defence of it, nor give countenance to any in taking such a step, and the Presbytery agree to drop the whole controversy concerning it.

2. That Mr. Clarke concur with this Presbytery in adhering to the National Covenant and the Solemn League, with the bond for renewing the same, together with the Act, Declaration and Testimony, as they were owned and professed before the unhappy division, and that he endeavor to prosecute the ends of them in his place and station.

3. That Mr. Clarke shall not endeavor to obtain a Presbytery in America constituted in opposition to this Presbytery, nor countenance any attempt towards erecting such a Presbytery.

4. That Mr. Clarke shall not preach upon an invitation from people who are in full communion with, or have made application to this Presbytery for sermon without their allowance, nor countenance any brother in taking such a step.

5. That Mr. Clarke shall acknowledge that this Presbytery, and Synod in Scotland to which it is subordinate, are lawful courts of Jesus Christ, and the Presbytery likewise acknowledge that the other Synod is a lawful court of Christ; nor do the Presbytery desire that he renounce his subjection to that Synod according to these terms.

6. That the members of this Presbytery shall not, either publicly or privately, justify the act condemning the Burgess Oath, or the censures passed against some of Mr. Clarke's brethren by their Synod, or justify any writing in defence of said censures, or countenance any step tending thereunto.

7. That the Presbytery and Mr. Clarke shall endeavor to strengthen one another in pursuance of these terms, and to bring about a general healing of the unhappy division in a Scriptural way.

8. That our secession, we must acknowledge, is such as is declared to be in the grounds of secession, contained in the first testimony, which is approved of and made judicial in the judicial testimony, and is substantially declared in our declinature, and so we look upon ourselves as standing upon the same footing as before the rupture.

9. That upon subscribing to these terms the Presbytery and Mr. Clarke shall, in the meantime and henceforward, maintain a brotherly communication with each other.

In witness whereof both parties have set their hands to this.

Subscribed by appointment.

ROBERT ANNAN, *Mod.*
THOMAS CLARKE.

SEPTEMBER 2, 1765.

Mr. Clarke was thus admitted, and the Presbytery had never any occasion to regret it, for he remained for nearly thirty years one of the most useful and honored presbyters of the church. And the Synod in Scotland appeared satisfied, for it never questioned the propriety and legality of the transaction.

In the spring of 1769 Rev. David Telfair, of Monteith, in Scotland, and Mr. Samuel Kinlock, probationer, arrived in Pennsylvania. They were both in connection with the Burgher Synod of Scotland, but, like Dr. Clarke, they applied immediately for membership in the Associate Presbytery of Pennsylvania. Their application was considered by Presbytery at its meeting in Neshaminy, and finally settled at a called meeting in Pequea, June 9, 1769. This meeting was called expressly "that steps might be taken for making the coalescence between this Presbytery and Mr. Telfair and Mr. Kinlock complete." The minute of this meeting runs thus: "They proceeded to consider the terms of agreement between them and the Rev. Thomas Clarke, of Stillwater, in the county of Albany, to which, with *some small variation*, the Rev. Mr. Telfair, minister of the gospel in Monteith, in Scotland, with Mr. S. Kinlock, probationer, did agree." What this "some small variation" was is nowhere given, and the presumption is that it was some verbal explanation; for we find the following subscription appended to the original Clarke covenant:

That the Rev. David Telfair, with Mr. Samuel Kinlock, having considered the above terms, approve of them, in testimony whereof he subscribed these presents.

DAVID TELFAIR,
SAMUEL KINLOCK.

JUNE 9, 1769.

When the news of this transaction reached Scotland there was a great outburst of indignation in the Anti-Burgher Synod. There were yet living many of the heroes of the great Burgher Oath fight of twenty years before, and the memory of their wounds and scars would not allow them to keep quiet. The meaning and expediency of an obscure Scotch oath must be a term of communion in the wilderness of the new world as well as in Scotland. Had they not turned their backs upon Ebenezer Erskine, the great leader of the Secession, and could they

now permit their foreign missionaries to fraternize with one of
his followers? Synod, at its meeting in 1770, condemned this
coalescence, and appointed three of their number to go as new
missionaries to America, and instructed them to require the
Presbytery to annul the union with the Burghers, and to obliterate their minute respecting it; and if the Presbytery refused to do so, then they and any of the brethren that choose
to join with them should constitute themselves into a new
Presbytery and hold no fellowship with the backsliders. The
Synod evidently held to the view that circumstances do not
alter cases—that Paul's law of expediency had waxed old and
had vanished away. The older members had come through
a long and fierce controversy, and, as a necessary result had become, to a large extent, impracticable theorists. The Presbytery, in its extra elaborate terms of union, had done a foolish
thing in specifying that the Burgher brethren were not to renounce subjection to their Synod. Subjection to the Presbytery was all that should have been required, and let the subordination of the Presbytery to its Synod take care of itself.
The members of Presbytery were not dependent upon either
Synod at home for their support, and their lives and doctrines
could not be reviewed Synodically, so that all subjection
amounted practically to very little. In reality it consisted
merely in depending upon Synod for more missionaries.

John Proudfit and James Ramsey declined going on this
mission, but John Smith of Sterling, volunteered to go with Mr.
John Rodgers. In the spring of 1771 Messrs. Rodgers and
Smith arrived at Philadelphia, and laid their instructions before Presbytery, at its meeting in Pequea, June 4th, 1771.
Did Presbytery obey these instructions and annul the union
and obliterate their minute? Strange to say, there is a doubt
upon this point, and, as we shall subsequently see, the popular
belief is most likely incorrect. Mr. Aiken, in his biographi-
cal sketch of Rev. John Cuthbertson, says, page sixteen: "Mr.
Telfair appears to have continued as a member of the Associate
Presbytery for about two years, when, by the action of the
Presbytery, the brethren who came in from the Burgher
Synod were *dismissed*. It is not definitely known with

whom Mr. Telfair held his ecclesiastical relations from 1771 to 1780." Dr. Beveridge, in the *Church Memorial*, page thirty-three, says: " The Presbytery agreed that the union with the Burgher brethren should be dissolved, as not consistent with their subordination to the Synod, and that they would have no further ministerial communion with them until the Synod should give them instructions. They declined erasing the minute relating to the union, judging the act of dissolving it sufficient. Messrs. Rodgers and Smith, considering the demands of Synod as materially complied with, took seats in the Presbytery, and the Synod appears to have been satisfied." The union of 1782 gave rise to a lively pamphlet warfare. One of these pamphlets, written by a ruling elder who was very familiar with the men and measures of that day, states the case thus: " These instructions they laid before Presbytery, when Dr. Mason, Mr. Marshall and others were present. The Presbytery viewed this as a very bold and rash step in that Synod, but imputed it to their ignorance of the state of the church here; and from this moment the Presbytery began to see clearly the danger of acknowledging any practical subordination to a Synod at such a distance, where they were not and could not be represented. The two gentlemen behaved prudently; they did not insist on their instructions, and the Presbytery without a dissenting voice, declared against obeying them. Mr. Marshall joined freely in this declaration with his brethren. Some considerable time after this Mr. Clarkson arrived in this country with much the same instructions, and they were also treated in much the same manner." When we turn to the minute of Presbytery itself, we find that it is so indefinite as to leave room for doubt, unless we look at it in the light of historic facts. The Presbyterial record is this, " The Presbytery met (at Mr. Proudfoot's house, in the evening of the 5th of June) and constituted with prayer, *ut supra sederunt* excepting the elder. They entered upon the consideration of the instructions given by the Synod to Messrs. Rodgers and Smith, and, after long reasoning on that head and application by a brother to the throne of grace for direction, they find that, in making the coalescence with the Burgher brethren, they have taken some steps inconsistent with their subordination to the Synod to which they have been and are subordinate, and they are determined that for the future they shall have no ministerial communion with them until they lay the case before the Synod and receive instructions from them. But they do not judge it for edification, in their present peculiar circumstances, explicitly to comply with the Synod's demand, which motion was unanimously agreed to by the Presbytery. And Mr. Rodgers and Mr. Smith, reckoning that the Synod's demand was materially granted, and being extremely loath to pursue any measures which might impede general edification, took their seats in the Presbytery." Dr. Beveridge supposed that the expression, "for the future they shall have no ministerial communion with them until they lay the case before the Synod and receive instructions," referred to the three Burgher ministers already received; but this could not be, because the Presbytery did not lay this case before Synod and wait instructions as that interpretation would require, for the case had been there already, and the Synod had given its instructions, and those instructions were just what was bothering Presbytery now, and it did not want any more of the same sort. Besides, as a matter of fact, the Presbytery never did withdraw "ministerial communion" from either Clarke, Telfair, or Kinlock, so that that interpretation would convict Presbytery of deliberate breach of promise. Presbytery admitted that there was something inconsistent in their action with their subordination to Synod, but their circumstances were anomalous; and these "peculiar circumstances" would not allow them "explicitly to comply with the Synod's demands," but that, in all *future* applications of Burgher ministers, they would withhold "ministerial communion" until they had referred the case to Synod, and had received its instruction. The minute will allow this construction, and we know that it is according to the facts of the case.

In 1770, Mr. Kinlock resigned his missionary appointment, received his certificate, and returned home to Scotland, and settled at Paisley. During the winter of 1770, or the spring of 1771, Mr. Telfair pulled up stakes and went back to Scotland without consulting Presbytery or asking its leave or certificate. Presbytery was so offended at this as to strike his name from its roll, and repudiate him for his insubordination. This left no Burgher minister in the Presbytery on the 4th of June, 1771, when Rodgers and Smith appeared with their instructions, excepting Thomas Clarke, of Salem, New York. If "ministerial communion" was withdrawn at all, it must have been from Mr. Clarke, alone; and yet it is an admitted historic fact, that Mr. Clarke's relations with his Anti-Burgher brethren were never disturbed. His right to a seat in Presbytery was never questioned. He remained an honored and useful member, in full communion with all the brethren, and in 1776, was set off with the Anti-Burghers, Mason and Annan, to constitute the new Presbytery of New York.

The subsequent action or non-action of Presbytery towards Mr. Telfair is consistent with this view. About 1773 or '74 he returned to this country; but he came as he went—unasked and unsent—and the Presbytery declined to restore him to his place, not because he was, or had been a Burgher, but because his course had been personally offensive. A writer of that day, who was subsequently a parishioner of Mr. Telfair, says: "Mr. Telfair's going back to Scotland and leaving the Presbytery in this embarrassed situation without any pressing call, as they thought; his going off without leave and without even asking a certificate, gave offence, and his returning again to America without any proper call or appointment, increased the offence, so that for some years he stood alone and was not admitted to communion with that body." Mr. Telfair remained in this isolated position, preaching in new settlements as he had the opportunity, and as stated supply of the old Burgher Church, in Shippen street, Philadelphia, which subsequently united with the Scott's Church, in Spruce street, till August 12, 1780, when he was received into the Reformed Presbytery, at its meeting at Stony Ridge, in Cumberland county, Pennsylvania, and came, with Cuthbertson, Lind and Dobbin, into the union of 1782, which formed the Associate Reformed Church.

The " present peculiar circumstances " which prevented their

explicit obedience to Synod, was the simple but stubborn fact
that the membership of every congregation in Presbytery was
composed of Burghers and Anti-Burghers, and if that old
Scotch oath controversy were started up in this country by ex-
pelling the Burgher ministers, it would rend every congregation, and at once call into existence an antagonistic Burgher
Presbytery. This they wished by all means to avoid, and the
third article of the terms of agreement was that the Burgher
brethren "should not endeavor to obtain a Presbytery in
America constituted in opposition to this Presbytery, nor
countenance any attempt towards erecting such a Presbytery."
Rodgers and Smith saw at once how things were, and did
not insist upon obedience to their instructions. They thought
that Presbytery had done right, and quietly took their seats
and said nothing more upon the subject, but worked on harmoniously with the brethren.

It is now impossible to tell how many of Mr. Cuthbertson's
preaching stations crystallized into regularly organized congregations, and at what times. We know that some did, and
some did not. Until the arrival of Messrs. Lind and Dobbin,
Mr. Cuthbertson regarded all the Covenanter settlements as belonging to his parish, even those in the State of New York,
upon the Walkill, in Orange county, and at Cambridge, in
Washington county.

At different times, a number of ruling elders were ordained
by him, but those of the same ordination did not all belong
to the same place—one would be from one station, and another
from a distant station—and they seemed to have a general, as well
as a local supervision. The first company of elders were ordained
at Rocky Spring, on the 8th of April, 1753, although George
Mitchell was the only one that lived there, while James and
George Wilson belonged to Licking Creek, and Jeremiah
Morrow and David Dinwiddie, to Rock Creek. In December
of the same year, he ordained several more at Octorara, who belonged to the stations east of the river. Again, in October,
1754, he ordained another company at the same place, among
whom was Walter Buchanan, of Stony Ridge. For several
years he held but one communion during the year, but this

was not for the benefit of any one place. A central location was selected during the pleasant weather of late summer or early autumn, and the members from all the stations were expected to be present and participate, and they were always received with a large and hearty hospitality by the resident families. The first communion, as already mentioned, was held at Stony Ridge, in August, 1752; the second was at Paxtang, in Dauphin county, October 14, 1753, when about two hundred communed; the third was at the same place, August 25, 1754, when about two hundred and fifty participated. Mr. Cuthbertson mentions in his diary that while engaged in prayer, asking a blessing upon the bread and wine, on this last occasion, a fearful thunder storm broke upon them, killing four horses and a dog some forty yards from the tent.

In the spring of 1773 either William or Benjamin Brown, of Paxtang, was sent as a commissioner to Ireland to procure two ministers, and was specially instructed to get, if possible, the Rev. Matthew Lind, pastor of the Covenanter congregation of Aghadowey, near Colraine, in Londonderry county. In his mission he was entirely successful. Alexander Dobbin, specially licensed and ordained for the purpose, and Mr. Lind returned with him, landing at Newcastle, Delaware, about the middle of December, 1773. At Paxtang, on the 10th of March, 1774, Messrs. Cuthbertson, Lind and Dobbin, with several elders, constituted themselves into the Reformed Presbyterian Presbytery of America. Mr. Cuthbertson resided at Octorara, and took charge of that church and Muddy Creek, in Lancaster county, and Lower Chanceford, in York county. Mr. Lind located in Paxtang, and assumed the pastorate of that church and Stony Ridge, in Cumberland county, with frequent visits to Sherman's Valley. Mr. Dobbin made his home at Rock Creek, now Gettysburg, and in addition to the care of that congregation, preached for four years part of his time at East Conecocheague, in Franklin county. None of the other mission stations formally organized during Mr. Cuthbertson's missionary supervision. The few families around Carlisle moved away, so that the station soon disappeared. Those near Newville kept up society meetings, with an occasional supply of sermon, but had neither house nor elder. They refused to go into the union of 1782, and subsequently coalesced with the scattered families around Green Village, Chambersburg and Green Castle, which took the same course, and when the Reformed Presbyterian Presbytery was re-constituted, and a church was formally organized on the Conecocheague, they were regarded as a wing of that pastoral charge. The clusters around Rocky Spring and upper East Conecocheague continued to receive occasional supplies, without any formal organization, beyond the presence of one ruling elder. Licking Creek, and the valley of the Great Cove Creek, after the first few years of Mr. Cuthbertson's itineracy, were rarely visited, because of their distance, and as the result, the former soon disappeared from notice, and the latter, with a kind of semi-organization, fraternized with the Associate congregation of West Conecocheague, and thus became a part of Mr. Rodgers' charge.

Mr. Rodgers, during his first summer in this country, spent most of his time among the churches west of the Susquehanna, and as a result, a call was presented to Presbytery, at its meeting at Oxford, November 12, 1771, from the churches at Conecocheague and Big Spring, for him to become their minister. A separate petition was also presented, "craving" his speedy admission among them. Mr. Rodgers accepted this call, "but he craved that it might be marked that, when he accepted the call of the people, it was with this view: That as soon as any one of the two places that had now put the call in his hand was able to support a minister, he should be disjoined from the other, as he reckoned it impracticable to have them both under his pastoral care for a long time, considering the distance of the one from the other." They were nearly thirty miles apart. Mr. Rodgers' installation did not take place before the summer of 1772, because of the lack of church buildings, and Presbytery, in April of that year, recommended these congregations "to erect decent places of worship with all convenient speed." Which recommendation was promptly complied with. The probabilities are that Mr. Rodgers preached one-half time in Big Spring and the other half in Franklin county, as one of the Humphreys papers shows that the Conecocheague churches paid him over seventy pounds per year, Pennsylvania currency, and it is not likely that the Big Spring congregation paid more.

The church at Big Spring was formally organized in September, 1764, when Rev. Matthew Henderson ordained and installed David Blean, George Espy, Robert Patterson, William Piper and John Sproat as ruling elders. The Conecocheague part of Mr. Rodgers' charge was composed of two organizations. One on the East and the other on the West Conecocheague, as all the new settlements were near to streams of water. Mr. Humphreys, of Mercersburg, has put into the hands of the writer a package of old papers which belonged to his father and his grandfather, both of whom were ruling elders in the Associate Reformed Church of West Conecocheague, and the latter as far back as 1772. These papers consist of old subscriptions for salary and scraps of minutes of congregational meetings, and are valuable in the absence of regular records. Mr. Rodgers, at the end of his first year's pastorate, desired to be released from the western part of his Franklin county charge. On the 21st of August, 1773, the West Conecocheague church had a meeting and adopted a remonstrance against this release, and sent it by Elder David Humphreys to Presbytery at Muddy Creek, on the 25th instant. In this remonstrance the following suggestive passage occurs: "We are as willing to support him and as high in subscriptions as any of the congregations, according to our number, taken in general; and were so in sending to Scotland, as some of the reverend Presbytery know; and we were with the first in petitioning the Synod at home; and were not the last in giving the ministers all the encouragement in our power. But if this takes place and we be cast off, after all our struggles to have the gospel in a stated way among us, we surely are worse in situation than ever, being cut off from the body. To set this matter in a clear light: In the first place, we are connected with our brethren of the Great Cove, and the nighest place of worship would be at so great a distance that the greatest part of us would be deprived altogether, except some few Sabbaths in the summer. Our agreement with the congregation of East Conecocheague was that we should have sermon according to

our subscriptions in proportion of their part; of which Mr.
Rodgers took a minute, and consented to come and preach to
us according to our proportion of time." This, in connection
with the headings of three or four subscription papers in the
Humphreys collection, reveals to us several things which bear
upon the origin and relations of these churches. That they
were among the first organized and were active in founding the
Secession church in this country; that there were two separate
and distinct organizations; that the people in the Cove had not
organized separately in 1774, but were still a constituent part
of the West church, and most likely received a part of its proportion of sermon somewhere within their own territory; and
that these churches must have had considerable strength and
prosperity to contribute over seventy pounds per year, a very
respectable sum for those days.

We know that Mr. Rodgers ministered once a month from
1772 to 1781, to the Associate Church of East Conecocheague,
and that Mr. Dobbin, of Gettysburg, ministered about as frequently, from 1774 to 1778, to the Reformed Presbyterian
Church of the same neighborhood; that both these churches
went into the union of 1782; and that they coalesced into one
congregation and became the East Conecocheague or Green
Castle branch of Matthew Lind's charge in 1783; but there is
no certainty as to the precise location of the meeting houses of
these two churches before their coalescence. There are circumstances which render it probable that the Covenanter
church was in the vicinity of Green Castle, and that the
Seceder church was near to the grave yard at Brown's Mills,
some four miles from Green Castle, where Mr. Lind lived, and
where he was buried.

The West Conecocheague church was located about a mile
and a half from Mercersburg on the road leading to Green
Castle. It stood upon a slate hill, and was generally known
familiarly as the Slate Hill Church. Because of the direction
of the roads near it, it was often called, even in Presbyterial
documents, the Corner. The building was, according to the
custom of that day, of logs, and was most probably erected in
the summer and autumn of 1772. The deed for the land upon

which it stands is dated December 10. 1777, in which William McCune conveys to the Trustees of the Associate congregation, one acre of land, with the privilege of a neighboring spring, for the sum of five shillings. The land is described as that upon which the church is already built. The brethren in the valley of the Cove had as yet no church building.

Of Mr. Rodgers' pastorate very little is now known, and even that little is not so much the result of positive information, as of logical inferences. He seemed to be a man of mild and amiable disposition, and was reasonably successful as a pastor; but he came into trouble from supposed unsoundness in doctrine.

At a meeting of Presbytery, held at Middle Octorara, October. 1777, it was resolved "That the Presbytery consider the case of Mr. Rodgers, of whom it is known that he has taught a number of tenets which the Presbytery judge not agreeable to our received principle. The Presbytery hereby order him to give his sentiments in a plain and inevasive manner to the next meeting, on the following heads, viz: Concerning the obligation of the Covenant of Works in Adam's posterity as to the positive and penal part; concerning mankind to have a legal right to common benefits; concerning Christ's yielding obedience to the preceptive part of the moral law, whether for Himself or His people; concerning Christ's purchasing blessings for His people."

Sickness prevented Mr. Rodgers from attending the next meeting of Presbytery, so Presbytery judicially condemned the doctrines he was supposed to hold without any personal reference to him, and cited him to appear at the next meeting. This he did, and seemed to satisfy the brethren, for his case was dismissed. But in Presbytery at Big Spring, May 29, 1779, his case was introduced anew, and again dismissed. At the next meeting at Pequea, it was introduced a third time, when "Presbytery proceeded to assert gospel truth in opposition to error said to be taught by Mr. Rodgers," and cited him to appear and answer at the next meeting. He appeared at Middle Octorara, May, 1780, and failed to satisfy the brethren. He then proposed to resign his seat in Presbytery, deliver up

pastoral charge, and desist from the exercise of his office till he
finally made up his mind upon the subject in dispute. What
an amazing proposition of forbearance, submission and non-re-
sistance for a Scotchman and an Anti-Burgher! But the majority of Presbytery agreed to it. Here, for the third time,
the matter was supposed to be ended. This shilly-shallying
of Presbytery for four or five years can be easily explained.
The Presbytery was very nearly divided upon the course to be
pursued, and when Mr. Rodgers' friends happened to be in a
majority at a meeting, his case was dismissed ; when his opponents chanced to be in the majority, then the case was brought
up again. So when Presbytery met at Marsh Creek, October,
1780, his opponents being in the majority, they resolved to
terminate the case judicially, and regularly libeled him, and
ordered the trial to be issued at Philadelphia, April 4. 1781. It
always happened that the further east the Presbytery met the
worse it was for him, for he had no friends in that end. In
the absence of himself and of the witnesses cited, the case was
issued, and on the 4th of April, 1781, he was " deposed from
the ministry, and excommunicated from the fellowship of the
church with the lesser sentence of excommunication." It was
further directed that this " sentence be intimated in the congregation of Big Spring by the minister who first supplies
there," and, " by the members of Presbytery in their respective
church, for the honor of truth and the information of the
people." This, of course, ended Mr. Rodgers' pastorate in Big
Spring and connections, but it was far from being the last of
his ministerial career. The ministerial vote in Presbytery
was: Affirmative—Clarkson, Henderson, Proudfit and Marshall. Negative—Logan, Murray and Smith. A year after
this, on the 12th of June, 1782, at Pequea, the Presbytery
finally adopted the Basis of Union, which resulted in the Associate Reformed Church. Against this, Clarkson and Marshall protested, and withdrew, and continued a Presbytery of
their own. This left Mr. Rodgers' friends in a majority in
the old Presbytery, and while there is no record upon the subject, yet the presumption is, that at that time, Mr. Rodgers was
restored to the ministry, for, in the following October, he ap-

peared as a member of the Presbytery, and took part in the first meeting of the Synod of the Associate Reformed Church.

The doctrinal errors with which he was charged, and for which he was deposed were, "That mankind, in their fallen state, are not under the law as a Covenant:—that the law written on Adam's heart, and the law given at Sinai, are two distinct laws:—that the latter is no part of the Covenant of Works:—that Christ did not purchase, by his obedience and death, any blessings of the Covenant and Grace." It is rather difficult to believe that Mr. Rodgers' was very much of an errorist in substance and reality, when men of such undoubted orthodoxy as Murray, Smith and Logan refused to condemn him.

On the 8th of April, 1753, David Dunwoody, grandfather of the late James L. Dinwiddie, D. D., and Jeremiah Morrow, father of the late Governor Morrow of Ohio, of Rock Creek, were ordained as ruling elders, and on the 13th of September, 1754, Mr. Cuthbertson "held sessions" there "rectifying disorders and removing differences." In the absence of more specific records, it may be safe to affirm that the Rock Creek congregation was organized on the 8th of April, 1753. It was composed entirely of Irish Covenanters who had settled there between 1740 and that date. It remained a part of Mr. Cuthbertson's general missionary charge till after the arrival of Mr. Dobbin and the organization of the Reformed Presbytery, when in 1774 he became its resident pastor, giving one-fourth of his time to the congregation near Green Castle. Mr. Dobbin was early and always a strong advocate of union with the Associate brethren, and doubtless impressed his spirit upon his people, for they went heartily with him into the union of 1782.

Marsh Creek, which flows a few miles west of Rock Creek, was also early settled by Irish, but they had been connected with the Secession Church. They were organized into a mission station just as soon as there were Associate ministers to look after them; most likely by Mr. Proudfit, who devoted his first four years in this country (1754-8) to such general missionary work. In October, 1762, Marsh Creek and a little branch on the Conewago gave a call to Robert Annan who was ordained and installed as their pastor on the 8th of June, 1763. This pastorate continued till April 21st, 1768, when Mr. Annan was released, and in the following year was installed in the churches on the Wallkill in Orange county, New York. Their next pastor was John Murray, of Scotland, who was ordained April 17, 1776, and installed November 2, 1777. He and his church came into the union of 1782 with much cordiality.

The township of Fermanagh, on the north side of the Juniata river in what is now Mifflin county, was early settled by Irish, of Secession antecedents, who looked to the Associate Presbytery for their religious teachers. A church was organized near the present Mexico, and in 1777 William Logan, who had arrived from Scotland in 1773, was installed as pastor of the congregation of Fermanagh and Racoon Valley. The latter was a small branch on the other side of the river. Pastor and people came into the union of 1782.

The congregation of Guinston, or Muddy Creek, York county, was settled between 1734 and '6, by families from both Scotland and Ireland. One of the earliest and most active settlers was Alexander Wallace from Scotland, whose great grandson now resides upon the original homestead. They were formally organized by Mr. Gellatly or Arnot, in the spring of 1754, by the ordination of Alexander Wallace, Thomas Currie, John Orr, William Orr, Samuel Harper and John McKay, as ruling elders. This Session was enlarged in May, 1769, by the addition of five more; and again in 1770 by another five. Soon after organization they erected a small log meeting house upon the same two acre lot which is occupied at present. In 1774 this was replaced by a stone building of thirty feet by forty-five. They made several efforts to procure a pastor, but were unsuccessful for nearly twenty years, during which time they were liberally supplied by the members of Presbytery, and especially by Proudfit and Henderson. They had considerable strength from the very beginning, for their subscription paper for salary in 1771 contained a hundred and thirteen male and two female subscribers, and amounted to nearly one hundred and three pounds. On the 25th of August, 1773, James

Clarkson, lately arrived from Scotland, was installed as their first pastor. He and the congregation declined to go into the union of 1782, and adhered to the residuary Associate Presbytery of Pennsylvania.

Mr. Cuthbertson preached his first sermon in Lower Chanceford on the 12th of December, 1751, and occasionally afterwards, until reinforced by the arrival of Lind and Dobbin. A church was not organized until March 27, 1771, when William Gebby and Daniel Sinclair were ordained as ruling elders. After the organization of the Reformed Presbytery and a distribution of its congregations among the three ministers, Lower Chanceford fell to the share of Mr. Cuthbertson, who supplied it, more or less, with the word and ordinances, as his increasing age and growing infirmities would permit, although he was never regularly installed as pastor; his relation was simply parental.

According to the testimony of Dr. Annan, the subject of union with the Reformed Presbytery was first introduced in the Associate Presbytery at a meeting at Marsh Creek in 1775, although no formal conference was held with the Reformed brethren for nearly two years. Various propositions were made and conventions held for five or six years, till, at a meeting of Presbytery in Pequea, Lancaster county, June 13, 1782, the basis of union was finally adopted. Messrs. Marshall and Clarkson, with their elders, protested and appealed to the Associate Synod of Scotland. These protestors withdrew, and Mr. Marshall, as clerk, retained the minutes, and they claimed to be the true Associate Presbytery of Pennsylvania.

One immediate result of this union was a bitter feeling between the parties and an active warfare of pamphlets. This is not the place to review this union work, but one or two remarks may be proper.

The difficulties in the way of a harmonious union arose perhaps as much from temperament and political feeling as from theological causes. The theological training of all the ministers had been the same, their minds had been literally run in the same mould, and even the forms of their expressions had been fashioned after the same model, so that it was not possible that there could be any great or essential difference of opinion as to dogma. They had worked together harmoniously thus far, and why not continue to do so still? To say that the movement was premature and that the church was not ripe for it, was to repeat just what had been said, and probably always will be said, of every such work. There are always and everywhere some so conservative by nature that they never ripen sufficiently to join in any forward enterprise. "The time is not yet," is their stereotyped answer, and if they are to be waited for, the time will never come. It was so in this union and it has been so in subsequent unions, both in Scotland, Ireland and the United States.

Political feeling was, beyond all question, a disturbing factor in the union of 1782. The efforts for a union were commenced about the time of the Declaration of Independence, they were carried on during the whole war, and the work was consummated just when we had gained our national cause. Everything during these six eventful years became saturated with one great desire for independence, which largely monopolized the minds of all men. Ministers felt it as strongly as did others. Drs. Mason and Annan were intense patriots, and both entered the army as volunteer chaplains. Such men could not brook the idea of a dependent church in a free State, and were just as eager and determined to throw off ecclesiastical subordination to Scotch Synods as to secure political independence of the British crown. There were others, however, who did not feel this desire for ecclesiastical autonomy, and were not willing to cut the cord which bound them to their mother church.

It is but just to add in this connection, as it can be, with pride and truthfulness, that every minister between the Susquehanna river and Fort Pitt, whether Presbyterian, Covenanter, or Seceder, sympathized with the Patriots in their struggle for independence. Some possessed more enthusiasm of nature, and showed more warmth and zeal than did others, yet they were all faithful to the cause. Mr. Cuthbertson, on the 2d of July, 1777, preached to a large congregation of Covenanters, from Jer. 4:2, "And thou shalt swear, The Lord liveth, in truth, in judgment, and in righteousness; and the nations shall bless themselves in Him, and in Him shall they glory;" and then led them in taking an oath of fidelity to the struggling colonies. Men who thus mixed their patriotism with their religion, could always be trusted.

The multiplication of churches during this period of planting would have been much greater had there been more laborers in the field. Some stations were without preaching for months, even years, and it is not possible to build up a cause, or even maintain a standing under such circumstances. Promising openings necessarily perished from neglect, and it is only a wonder that so many churches struggled up into a healthy existence. The few ministers that were secured for the field were men of good ability, of excellent culture, and devoted to their laborious work, and met the demands of the field as far as possible, and the settled congregations were very generous, and allowed their pastors to devote a large share of their time to destitute places.

As an illustration of the ways by which our fathers met the difficulties of their situation, it may be worth noting, that from 1780 to '82 or '3, the congregations in Franklin county, and most likely elsewhere, subscribed for "stipends," so many bushels of wheat, or the current value thereof, instead of pounds or dollars. The Government had issued so much paper money to meet the exigencies of the war, that there was no longer any prospect of its being redeemed, and just as soon as the public became convinced of this fact, this "Fiat Money" began to depreciate so rapidly, that in a short time, it became worthless, notwithstanding the Government's promise to pay. It ceased to be a medium of trade, for it had no fixed value, and men had to fall back to the moneyless system of barter and exchange, and make the bushel of wheat the measure of values, for it had an intrinsic worth. There are principles in political economy just as fixed and unvarying as the laws of matter, or the rules of morality, and it is not only our privilege, but our duty, to learn wisdom from the failures as well as the successes of our fathers.

CHAPTER II.

1782 to 1822.

THE Associate Reformed Synod, at its first meeting in Philadelphia, October 31, 1782, re-arranged the Presbyteries according to territory, and made Messrs. Henderson, Lind, Rodgers, Dobbin, Logan, Murray, and the churches in West Pennsylvania, to constitute the *Second Associate Reformed Presbytery.* The Susquehanna river was the dividing line between East and West Pennsylvania. In 1786, the Synod changed the name of this Presbytery to that of the *Presbytery of Pennsylvania.* In 1793, it was divided by the Synod, and the portion west of the Allegheny mountains was erected into the *Second Presbytery of Pennsylvania,* and the eastern part was designated as the *First Presbytery of Pennsylvania.* In 1802, the Synod decreed the organization of four particular Synods, viz: The Synod of the Carolinas, composed of the First and Second Presbyteries of the Carolinas; the Synod of Scioto, composed of the Presbyteries of Kentucky and Monongahela; the Synod of Pennsylvania, composed of the Presbyteries of Philadelphia and Big Spring; and the Synod of New York, composed of the Presbytery of New York and Washington. Also, that there should be an annual General Synod, composed pro rata of delegates from all the Presbyteries. It was ordered that the Presbytery of Big Spring consist of Rev. Messrs. William Logan, John Young, Thomas Smith, James Walker, James McConnell, William Baldridge and James Harper, Jr., with their elders; and that the Presbytery shall meet at Mr. Logan's Church, the Fermanagh Church, on Wednesday, the 18th of May, 1803, and be opened with a sermon by the Rev. Mr. Logan. By this arrangement, all the ministers and churches between the Susquehanna river and the Allegheny mountains were placed in the Presbytery of Big Spring, except those of the counties of York and Adams, which were attached to the Presbytery of Philadelphia. After the re-organization of the Presbytery of Big Spring, by the Synod of the West, in 1825, it was left without any definite ,boundary on the east, inasmuch as the Synod had no other territory east of it. At the union of 1858, it was made to embrace the territory between the Susquehanna and the Allegheny mountains.

The attention of the Presbytery was so entirely taken up with the care of its churches, that it has no separate and distinct history, so that a brief account of congregational histories will tell the whole story of its labors, of its sorrows and of its successes.

STONY RIDGE.

With the exception of Mr. Clarkson and his church at Guinston, all the ministers and congregations between the Susquehanna and the Allegheny mountains joined the union and became Associate Reformed in 1782. This was followed with the happiest results, for small congregations in the same neighborhood united into one, and new and better combinations were made for pastoral charges. In the summer of 1783 Matthew Lind received and accepted a call to the churches in Franklin county. His removal from Paxtang and Stony Ridge had become a necessity for these churches were never strong, especially the latter, and as soon as the war of independence was substantially over, the German population began to move westward in great numbers. They literally crowded out the Irish, and in a few years both congregations were completely exterminated, so completely that there is scarcely a tradition of their existence left among the present inhabitants. Although the Paxtang church does not fall within the scope of this history, yet, its close relation and occasional incidental notice present a temptation too strong to resist, to turn aside for a little, and note a marked instance of the covenant fidelity and loving kindness of our God, who said to Abraham, and through him to all believers, " I will establish my covenant between me and thee, and thy seed after thee, in their generations, for an everlasting covenant, to be a God unto thee, and to thy seed after thee."

When Graham of Claverhouse was raiding the west of Scot-

3

land with fire and sword in 1685, he seized John Brown, the
pious carrier of Muir Kirk parish, while working in the field,
and brought him to his own door, and said "John, go to your
prayers, for you shall immediately die." The martyr neither
asked for mercy nor length of days, but kneeled down and
poured out his heart in language so affecting, that the soldiers,
profane and hardened as they were, were moved almost to
tears. After kissing his wife and two infant children, Claverhouse ordered the soldiers to fire. But the prayers of the good
man had so affected their hearts that they decidedly refused to
have a hand in his death. The villianous commander, utter-
ing an angry oath, shot him with his pistol and rode away.
The widow laid her babe upon the ground, gathered up the
scattered brains of her murdered husband, bound up his head
with her apron, covered his body with her plaid, and sat down
and wept. For her there seemed to be no to-morrow. But God
soon found means to hide her and her little ones safely away
in Ireland. In process of time one of these infants was permitted to rejoice over six pious sons; all of whom emigrated
to America about 1740, or shortly afterwards, and settled a
few miles east of where the city of Harrisburg now stands,
and became the nucleus of the Covenanter church of Paxtang,
in the eldership of which two or three of them long served,
The late Dr. Matthew Brown, of Jefferson College, in relating
these things to the writer, said that "these six brothers were
princes in Israel, for they were men of prayer, and had power
with God." When the Paxtang church was crowded out as already mentioned, these brothers scattered; one went to Centre
county and gave to the ministry of the word, his son, Dr. Matthew Brown, who in his turn gave sons and grandsons to the
same work. Another removed to Big Spring and two of his
great-grandsons and a great-grandson-in-law are ministers in
the United Presbyterian church. Another found his home in
Washington county, and through his son-in-law, Dr. Gilbert Mc-
Masters, gave more ministers to the Church of Christ. And it
was doubtless so with others of the six brothers. Thus the
wrath of man designed to quench the influence of the piety of
John Brown, but it was overruled by God, so as to result in

a wide dispersion and marvelous multiplication of pious agency and power.

Walter Buchanan was the only elder in Stony Ridge when Mr. Lind was installed. About that time Joseph Junkin was ordained. He lived upon the present Kanaga farm, built its present stone house, and had "the tent" upon it during his life time. It is not certainly known that there was any other elders. This little church was always a colony, surrounded by a population which had no sympathy with them; and after the removal of Mr. Lind and some of the families, there was but little motive left for the others to remain. They could sell their lands for a good price and go west and purchase where land was cheaper and religious privileges more to their wishes. Presbytery sent them some supplies, but as the families became fewer the supplies diminished until the station was wholly abandoned. The Bells, and the Swansies, and the Junkins temporarily attached themselves to the Big Spring congregation, but in time they too passed away, and not a single descendant of the original stock is now known to reside in the neighborhood. Joseph Junkin, Jr., son of the elder, moved in 1806 to Mercer, Mercer county, and helped to found the Associate Reformed church in that place, and served in its eldership for years. One of his daughters married Rev. James Galloway, Mercer's first pastor; another married Rev. George Buchanan, of Steubenville; and another married John Findley, an elder of Mercer, all of whom gave sons to the ministry of the Associate Reformed church. His sons, Drs. George and David X., also served long and well as leading men of the Presbyterian church.

And thus it has continued to be to the present day; our loss in the East was always gain to the church in the West. Congregations in the process of becoming extinct here, have founded new and strong churches there. Some of the congregations in this Presbytery have run down very much in numerical strength, others have been entirely blotted out, yet, in no instance has this occurred because the members have yielded their religious convictions or changed their theological faith, but because, for economical reasons, they have felt compelled

to move to some other section of the country. The Germans
of Eastern Pennsylvania, more plodding and thrifty, and less
venturesome and enterprising than the Scotch-Irish, have, for
the past century, steadily pressed across the Susquehanna, and
refused to pass the Alleghenies; and have thus gradually, and
to a very considerable degree, crowded out the descendants of
the original settlers. These Germans are moral and religious
people, and make good citizens, but they always brought their
own churches with them, and so made very little use of those
they found. They knew not Calvin, or Knox, or Cameron, or
Erskine, but followed after Zwingle, or Luther, or Zinzendorf,
or Menno, or Otterbein, or Winebrenner, or Albright.

FRANKLIN COUNTY.

In 1783, Matthew Lind was installed pastor of the United
Congregations of Green Castle, Chambersburg, West Conecocheague, and the Great Cove. The Green Castle church was a
union or combination of the Reformed and Associate churches
of the neighborhood previous to the union of 1782. For a
time they worshiped as best they could in the two little old
log meeting-houses, but the enlargement of the congregation
by the union, and its subsequent prosperity, soon rendered the
old accommodations entirely insufficient. In 1782 the town of
Green Castle was laid out by Colonel John Allison, and within
ten years quite a little village sprung up. In May, 1791, John
Gebby, George Clark, Andrew Reed, John Coughran and James
Crooks, trustees of the Associate Reformed church of Green
Castle, bought of James McLanahan and John Allison, a lot
at the east side of the town, on Baltimore street, where the old
grave-yard now is, and erected a large log building, ceiled and
painted inside, and weather-boarded and painted white outside.
It was comfortably fitted up, and was always known in the
town as the *White Church*, to distinguish it from the Presbyterian *Red Church*. Here the Associate Reformed Synod met
in 1799, which formed and adopted the "Standards" of that
church; and here, in May, 1804, was held the first meeting of
the General Synod; and it became a favorite meeting place for
Synods and Presbyteries; and for many years it was one of the

most active and prosperous churches in the Presbytery. At the time of the union in 1782, the session was composed (upon the authority of tradition) of James McLanahan, William Gebby, Andrew Reed, David Fullerton, George Clark and Joseph Gebby. It is not known how they had been previously divided between the Reformed and Associate churches, or how many of them had served from the organization of those churches.

On the 21st of April, 1800, the Rev. Matthew Lind died, in the fortieth year of his ministry, and in the sixty-ninth year of his age. He was born at Cairn Castle, in the county of Antrim, Ireland, of Scotch parents; was educated at Glasgow University, and was licensed and ordained by the Reformed Presbytery of Scotland. He was for thirteen years pastor of the Reformed Presbyterian church of Aghadowey, in the county of Londonderry, Ireland. He came to this country in 1773, at the solicitation of a special delegation sent to Ireland, and for nine years took the charge of the Paxtang and Stony Ridge churches, and spent the remainder of his ministry in Franklin county. In 1797 he was thrown from his horse, and so injured as to be no longer able to discharge fully the duties of his position, and during the next year sought and obtained the dissolution of his pastoral relation. In person he was large and rather corpulent, was comely in appearance, and possessed mild and winning manners. His friend and immediate successor, John Young, says: "He was a laborious student all his life, and rarely, if ever, appeared in the pulpit without giving ample proof of his being master of his subject. * * * Often have crowded auditories had their attention astonishingly riveted for hours together, whilst with singular ability he has unfolded the sublime mysteries of the gospel and traced the various exercises of the Christian life. * * * In private life he was an ornament to the Christian character, and recommended the doctrines which he publicly taught by the silent energy of an eminently holy example."

In 1799 John Young was installed pastor of Green Castle, West Conecocheague and the Great Cove, and gave good promise of great usefulness in this wide field. But his race was soon run, for he died on the 24th of July, 1803, in the prime of his manhood, and to the great grief of his congregations and of the Church at large.

Mr. Young was born September 4, 1763, in York county, of Covenanter parentage, was graduated at Dickinson College in 1788, and studied theology mainly with Dr. Nisbet, president of the college; he was licensed in 1790 by the Presbytery of Pennsylvania, and on the 20th of August, 1792, was ordained and installed as pastor of the Timber Ridge and Old Providence churches in Virginia. He was a man of good abilities, of fine mental culture and of affable manners, and was always heard with gladness. While he was not capable of making those occasional brilliant efforts which Dr. Mason sometimes did, yet it was the opinion of Dr. McJimsey and others, who knew both parties well, that as a steady every-day preacher he was fully the doctor's peer. His son, Dr. John C. Young, of Centre College, was one of Kentucky's most eloquent and useful men. His grandson, William Young, is now pastor of an important church in Chicago.

On the 5th of October, 1808, John Lind, son of the Rev. Matthew, was ordained by the Big Spring Presbytery, at Green Castle, and installed as pastor of the churches of Green Castle, Hagerstown, West Conecocheague and the Great Cove. He was a popular preacher, a wise pastor and an amiable man, and his labors were crowned with a blessing.

So strong did the Green Castle and Hagerstown churches become, that at a meeting of Presbytery at Concord, on the third Tuesday of June, 1817, they presented a petition for his separation from West Conecocheague and Great Cove, and the devoting of his entire services to them. This petition was granted, and in this reduced charge, he continued to labor with increasing ability and success, until the period of his death, respected and loved by all who knew him.

The church of West Conecocheague was but little strengthened by the union of 1782, as there were not many Covenanters within its immediate bounds. But it experienced a fair measure of success during the pastorate of the elder Lind. In 1796 they expended seventy-three pounds in repairing their church building, when they ceiled it, and re-seated it, and put in it a new pulpit, and weather-boarded and painted it exteternally.

But the tide of their prosperity seemed to have attained its greatest height about this period, for adverse influences now set in. In 1786 the town of Mercersburg was laid out, and soon became a centre of population, and the Presbyterian church, which was located two miles and a half in the country, saw the advantages of the position, and in 1794 moved into the growing town, and under the wise administration of the excellent and able Dr. King, greatly prospered. Inasmuch as these two churches were precisely the same in doctrine, government and forms of religious worship, many could see no good reason why the one should be preferred to the other, and for convenience sake, fell in with the village church; and thus a stream, small indeed, but yet sensibly felt, turned away from the other's door. A church thus located near to a village, but too far away for the villagers, is always depleted, and in the end is pretty sure to succumb to its town competitor.

The church not only lost in this way its mechanics and tradespeople who kept no horses, but the farming population became restless and unsettled under a spirit of western emigration, which became very rife about the beginning of the present century. Even the unquestioned ability of John Young and John Lind was unable to repair the loss of this double depletion, and the church run slowly but steadily down till 1817, when Mr. Lind resigned its charge. This left it in a very helpless condition, for it could not combine with other churches to form a new pastorate, and it could get but little supply from Presbytery, for the General Synod had become very much enfeebled under the discouragement and distractions of the Mason controversies, and had but little supply to distribute. It had still three good elders, Henry Anderson, James Clark, and David Humphreys, and a band of very reliable members. But what could they do? They had no prospect of ever having another pastor, and were not able to procure any supply beyond an occasional Sabbath. They became disheartened, and gave themselves over to the disintegration of time. They preserved

their organization till the disastrous union of 1822 broke up
the Presbytery.

The presumption is, that the church never formally disbanded, but just melted away and ceased to exist. Some
joined the Presbyterian church, some identified themselves
with the Associate church that was struggling up into existence in Mercersburg, some moved away, and others remained for
a time just as they were. The old meeting-house on Slate Hill
remained tenantless for years, and was then sold and removed
to another place and erected, and now does service as a dwelling house. Nothing remains to recall the story of the past except the old grave yard, where sleep the accumulated dead of
a hundred years, sealed by the holy Spirit of God unto the day
of redemption. The children are gone but the parents still remain to tell what has been.

Big or Great Cove Creek in the eastern edge of Fulton
county heads a short distance north of McConnellsburg, and
runs down a narrow valley between the Cove mountain and
Scrub Ridge, and unites with Licking Creek before it empties
into the Potomac. It was early settled by Irish Covenanters,
to whom were subsequently added some Irish Seceders and
Synod of Ulster families. Being too few in numbers to do
much in the way of supplying themselves with church privileges they early connected themselves with the Seceder church of
West Conecocheague to which access was had through Cove
Gap, and thus remained an integral part of that church during
the pastorate of Mr. Rodgers. But when Mr. Lind was installed in 1783, they constituted one of the four organized
branches of his pastoral charge. Of the time and circumstances of their formal organization as a separate church, no
record or account can be found; but the presumption is that
they were so organized in 1783, in anticipation of the installation of Mr. Lind. It is not known how much of Mr. Lind's
services was received by this congregation, for the uniform
custom in this charge was that each branch received in proportion to what it paid, and the probability is that the Great
Cove did not receive the one-fourth of his time.

This congregation was never numerically strong, indeed it

could not be, because the territory which it covers was so restricted and hemmed in with mountains as to limit the number of its population. But the same cause gave stability and uniformity to its history, so that year after year it remained very much the same. Hid away among the mountains it felt but little the influences of popular excitements, and consequently experienced but few and slight changes.

It is known that their meeting place was for some time in McConnellsburg, and at other times further down the valley. As the territory occupied by the congregation was long and narrow it is probable that for reciprocal convenience they met at different places, and it is possible that they had two houses, one for each end of the congregation. Having enjoyed the pastorates of Matthew Lind, John Young and John Lind, they became vacant in 1817 by the resignation of the last. They did not however become discouraged by their change after enjoying the word and ordinances so long, but sought and occasionally obtained supplies so long as the Presbytery could look after them.

A number of Covenanter and Seceder families early located in the neighborhood of Chambersburg, who received an occasional sermon from passing ministers, but they were regarded as belonging to the churches organized at or near Green Castle, from which they were distant only ten or twelve miles. When the union of 1782 made it possible to settle a minister in Franklin county, they took the proper measures to become a part of Matthew Lind's new charge. The circumstances of their case make it probable that their formal organization took place at this time, the summer of 1783, and in view of the settlement of Mr. Lind. They had a house of worship at an early period of their history, for in the contract for repairing the meeting house of West Conecocheague, it is stipulated that the new pulpit shall be modeled after and as good as Mr. Lind's pulpit in Chambersburg.

When Chambersburg was rendered vacant by the resignation of Mr. M. Lind, it joined with the church in Shippensburg, and called James Walker, who was ordained and installed over these two congregations on the 4th of September, 1799. Mr.

Walker resigned his pastorate on the the 8th of August, 1820, and moved west. Thomas N. Strong was ordained and installed as his successor on the 23d of October, 1821, and his short pastorate brought them down to the distractions of the union of 1822.

Hagerstown was for many years a preaching station before it attempted anything like a formal organization. This immediate section of country was early settled by Germans, principally of the Reformed connection, and the Irish population was not sufficiently numerous to maintain church ordinances in their midst. Then there were Presbyterian and Associate Reformed churches within ten miles, with which they were associated, and where they attended more or less frequently.

In the year 1737, the Presbytery of Donegal sent Samuel Caven, an Irish licentiate, into the region of southern Franklin county, and the neighboring border of Maryland. In 1739, he was ordained and installed over the congregations of East Conecocheague, which embraced the whole section from Chambersburg to Maryland. He got into trouble with the northern part of his large parish, and finally had himself dismissed from his charge and Presbytery; but he continued to preach upon his own responsibility in Green Castle, and the region south of it, until 1750. In 1754, Rev. John Steel entered and served in this region for about two years, when the Indian troubles connected with the Old French war forced him to leave. For the next nineteen years nothing was done for Presbyterianism in this territory. In 1774, the Rev. Thomas McPherrin accepted a call to the united congregations of East and West Conecocheague and Jerusalem. By Jerusalem, the region about Hagerstown was intended, as the town of Hagerstown was not laid out until 1777 or '8. This pastoral relation was dissolved in 1779. Nothing farther was attempted till 1788, when a Mr. Caldwell was appointed by Presbytery to supply "for one year" at Falling Water, Hagerstown and Williamsport. This was the last movement which the Presbyterians made towards the securing or supplying of Hagerstown. In 1783 Mr. Matthew Lind became pastor of the neighboring Associate Reformed churches in Franklin county,

and when we consider the destitution of the place, the missionary character of his ministry, and the fact that he acquired members of his Green Castle church from that region,
it is more than probable that he occasionally preached in Hagerstown. The same condition of affairs continued during
the short pastorate of Mr. Young, and during more than half
the pastorate of Mr. J. Lind. And yet no movement towards
a church organization was made till 1817. The Presbyterians
of the place were members of the church in Green Castle, or
at Welsh Run, and the Associate Reformed families were connected with the Green Castle church. The Germans constituted the major part of the community, and had organizations,
both Reformed and Lutheran, in the town. The Associate
Reformed element must have gained considerable strength, for
the call which was given to Mr. J. Lind in 1808, was from the
united congregations of Green Castle, Hagerstown, West Conecocheague and the Great Cove. Mr. Lind preached regularly
in Hagerstown during his entire pastorate, and for nine years
held his services in the German Reformed building, as his
father and Mr. Young had done before him. In 1817, they
built of brick their first meeting-house, which remained till
a few years ago, and then took measures to be separated from
Green Castle, and to be formed into a distinct congregation.

On Saturday, the 15th of November, 1817, Robert Douglass,
John Kennedy, Joseph Gabby and John Robertson were ordained by Mr. Lind as ruling elders in the Associate Reformed
church of Hagerstown. Whether they were chosen by the
residents of that place, or were selected by the session of Green
Castle, the records do not show. After their ordination they
received to the membership of the church in Hagerstown the
following persons, who were members in Green Castle, viz:
Robert and Sarah Douglass, John and Margaret Kennedy,
Joseph and Ann Gabby, Hugh Kennedy, John Robertson,
James McCulloch, John and Sarah Johnston, David and Ann
Johnson, Mrs. Sarah Simpson, Mrs. Susan Dowing, Peggy
Johnson, Jane Milligan and Maria Kerr. And upon personal
examination, John and Ann Gibbons, Nancy Douglass, Mary
Douglass, William Robertson, Samuel Steel, Elizabeth Steel,

Susanna Bell, Rosanna White, James Ferguson, James O. Carson, John and Nancy McElhenny, Alex. McNeil and Dr. S. Young. On certificate from Presbyterian churches, Mrs. Susanna Bell, Mrs. D. Hoyt, Mrs. Ann Hughes, Mr. and Mrs. Farquar and David Cook. In all thirty-nine. On the next day their new church was used for the first time, when the Lord's Supper was dispensed. This communion season was enjoyed with peculiar pleasure, because, although Presbyterians had preached there for eighty years, it was the first dispensation of the Lord's Supper in Hagerstown by Presbyterian hands. In view of this organization, and for the purpose of cultivating this field more thoroughly, Mr. Lind had, a month or two before, resigned his charge of West Conecocheague and the Great Cove. And during the remainder of his life, he divided his time equally between Green Castle and Hagerstown.

THE VALLEY OF VIRGINIA.

The first settlers in Virginia were Englishmen of the Cavalier school, who believed strongly in the Divine right of kings and of diocesan bishops, and as a natural result the early colony became more intolerant, in both church and State, than was England under the régime of the Stuarts, and far exceeded anything caricatured in the spurious Blue Laws of Connecticut. Democratic Presbyterianism was not allowed, for a century, to find a resting-place among the haughty planters of the Old Dominion. In 1618 they enacted a law, that "every person should go to church on Sundays and on holy days, or lie neck and heels that night and be a slave to the colony the following week." For the second offense he was to be a "slave for a month," and for the third offense he was to be in bondage "for a year and a day." In 1642, the very time when the prelatical hierarchy was subverted in Britain, it was enacted that "no minister shall be permitted to officiate in this country but such as shall produce to the Governor a testimonial that he hath received his ordination from some bishop in England; and shall then subscribe to be conformable to the orders and constitution of the Church of England; and if any other person, pretending himself to be a minister, contrary to this act, shall presume to teach or preach, publicly or privately, the Governor or council are hereby desired and empowered to suspend and silence the person so offending ; and upon his obstinate persistence, to compel him to depart the country with the first convenience."

When the Hanover-Brunswick family came to the throne, colonial persecution relaxed a little, and a number of Irish Presbyterians, landing at Newcastle and Baltimore, gradually found their way up the Shenandoah river, and quietly settled in the valleys among the mountains. Still, even then and there, their annoyances were such that the Synod of Philadelphia, in 1738, interceded with Mr. Gooch, then Lieutenant-Governor of Virginia, on behalf of "their scattered brethren who resided west of the Blue Ridge." Mingled in this stream of Irish were many Dissenters, who turned at once to the Associate Presbytery of Pennsylvania for their religious privileges. We have now no means of knowing how many churches were organized and preaching places established before the union of 1782, in this section of country. There were at least two or three, for in 1783, John Rodgers, late of Big Spring, was installed as pastor of the united congregations of Timber Ridge, in Rockbridge county, and Old Providence, in Augusta county. These churches had evidently existed for some time, as they had acquired permanence and strength sufficient for the support of a minister, and the neighborhood had been pretty well settled before the Revolution.

Mr. Rodgers was not destined to enjoy peace, for trouble soon sprung up and found its way into the courts of the church. In 1789 a Synodical commission, consisting of Dobbin, Boyse and Smith, was sent down to investigate matters; and the final result was, that in 1790 Mr. Rodgers was suspended from the ministry by the Synod, for "errors in doctrine and immorality in conduct." It is nowhere stated what these were, but from what had taken place previously we can readily surmise at least in part. Mr. Rodgers never again sought restoration to the ministry. He was a native of Crieff, at the foot of the Grampians in Scotland, was educated at St. Andrew's College, and to his scientific and theological education he added a thorough Scotch course in medicine. After his appointment by Synod as a missionary to this country, he married, October 1, 1770, Elizabeth Blackwood, of gentle and wealthy parentage, and soon afterwards sailed, accompanied by Mr. Smith. After a long and rough voyage they landed and reported to Presbytery as already narrated. He was a man of gentle spirit, fair abilities, and thorough education. When finally suspended from the ministry, he turned his attention exclusively to medicine, and became a very successful practitioner. He died and was buried, in 1812, at Tinker Ridge, Va., where he had lived for twenty-nine years. His Scotch wife died during his first pastorate, and lies buried in the parcel of ground which she had donated to the Big Spring congregation for a burying place. He married a second wife, Isabella Ireland, in Cumberland county, and left to his adopted country eight sons and two daughters, a number of whose descendants are worthy United Presbyterians. Four of his children settled and died at Gallipolis, Ohio, three others settled on farms within five miles of Monmouth, Illinois, one died at Xenia, one at Chillicothe, and another in Michigan. Six of his great-great-grandchildren are members of our church in Mercer, Pa., and one of his great-grandsons is a ruling elder there.

In August, 1792, John Young was ordained and installed as pastor of Timber Ridge and Old Providence, and discharged his duties with great acceptance till the summer of 1799, when he resigned, and removed to Green Castle, Pa. It was a long time before either of these congregations was permitted again to see the face of a pastor. The Timber Ridge congregation became associated for a season with the church in the Forks of the James River, and the Rev. William Baldridge served them as a stated supply from 1803, till June, 1809, when he accepted a call to Cherry Forks and connections in Adam county, Ohio, under the care of the Presbytery of Kentucky, where he lived many years, and did a good work for the church. For eleven years Timber Ridge depended upon occasional supply, till June 1820, when Rev. James Brown, late of Concord, commenced to preach there and at Old Providence. They gave him a call

as pastor, but it is believed that he was never installed, and
that he remained for only a couple of years. This terminated
all connection between Timber Ridge and this Presbytery.
The presumption is that after the crash of 1822 they sought
supply from the first Presbytery of the Carolinas. In 1840, the
Associate Presbytery of the Carolinas was destroyed because
of the antagonism between its Synod and the peculiar institution of the South, and Rev. Horatio Thompson, a native of
Cambridge, New York, who was connected with it, soon afterwards joined the Associate Reformed Synod of the South, and
located near to Timber Ridge, and eventually became its pastor,
and has so continued to the present time.

On the 15th of November, 1804, William Adair was received as a probationer from the Presbyterian church, and for
more than two years supplied in Mifflin county, Pennsylvania,
and among the churches in the Valley, principally at Old Providence. On the 7th of April, 1807, he was ordained at Newville, Pennsylvania, and at the same meeting of Presbytery received and accepted a call from the churches at Old Providence
and Sinks, in Monroe county. From different causes his installation never took place, but he labored in these places till
the 19th of April, 1809, when he was released from Old Providence, and that portion of his time was given to churches in
Greenbrier county. His main reasons for this were the distance of a hundred miles between Monroe and Old Providence,
and the difficulties intervening, which he enumerated as six
large rivers, innumerable creeks, and three high mountains,
over one of which there was no regular road. Old Providence
received no more stated supply till the summer of 1820, when
the Rev. James Brown took charge of it and Timber Ridge
for two or three years as already narrated. After the re-organization of the Presbytery in 1825, Old Providence alone of
all the churches in the Valley of Virginia returned to it, and
sought and received supplies, more or less steadily till the 19th
of April, 1844, when it was formally transferred to the First
Associate Reformed Presbytery of the South, and then re-
joined its old associate at Timber Ridge, and has ever since remained as a part of Dr. Thompson's pastorate.

The church in the Forks of the James River, in Rockbridge county, is mentioned in the records of the church very soon after the union of 1782, and is probably as old as its neighbor at Timber Ridge. Its first pastor was the Rev. William Baldridge, who was ordained and installed in August, 1793. Because of their inability to support him he resigned the pastorate on the 18th of October, 1803, although he continued to minister to it, in connection with Timber Ridge, as stated supply, till the summer of 1809. From this time it depended upon occasional supplies sent them till the disorganization of Presbytery in 1822, after which it identified itself with the Associate Reformed Synod of the South, and constitutes at present, the writer thinks, a pastorate of the same under other names and new organizations.

In the spring of 1806 a petition was received from a society at the Sinks, in Monroe county, Virginia, asking to be received under the care of Presbytery, signed by two ruling elders and other members, accompanied by a liberal subscription paper signed by seventy-five heads of familes and thirty other persons. These came from an old organized church which had trustees and elders and more than a hundred communicants, but there is no record to show what their antecedent connection had been. In April, 1808, a petition, signed by over sixty names, was received from "the inhabitants about Sinking Creek, Greenbrier county," asking to be recognized as "a church under your care," "being desirous to have the Gospel preached amongst us, more according to the principles of the Reformation than hitherto we have had it; and being favored with a copy of the testimony published by the Associate Reformed Synod, and being perfectly satisfied with the principles of your church." At the same time another petition, couched in the same words, from "The church on Antonic's Creek, Greenbriar county, Virginia," and making the same request, was presented, and both churches were received. There was no subsequent organization in either case, showing that they came in a fully organized form, from some other, but now unknown, ecclesiastical connection.

As stated elsewhere, in 1807, Mr. Adair accepted a call

from the Sinks and Old Providence, but was never installed in either. After his release from Old Providence, in 1809, he gave one-half of his time to the churches on Sinking Creek and on Antonie's Creek, in Greenbrier county. Mr. Adair continued to serve these three churches as stated supply till November 22, 1813, when the Sinks church asked that they might be released from their relation to him, whatever that relation may be, inasmuch as he had never been regularly installed as their pastor. Presbytery granted them their request, and Mr. Adair continued during the subsequent winter with the Greenbrier churches. The minutes of Presbytery under date of May 25, 1814, have this brief record: "Received and read a petition from the Rev. William Adair, soliciting permission to cease from discharging the functions of the Gospel Ministry; and on motion,

"*Resolved*, That the prayer of the above petition be and it is hereby granted."

The reasons for this request are not here given, but the prompt and indulgent action of the Presbytery evidently shows that error in doctrine, or immorality in conduct, could not have been involved, for they would have been met with discipline, instead of a peaceful secularization.

These churches, particularly the Sinks, continued to receive supply from Presbytery, but finally disappeared in the breaking up of 1822. There is now a church in Monroe county in connection with the Associate Reformed Synod of the South, but whether it has had any relationship with the old Sinks church, the writer has no means of knowing.

In May, 1804, a church on Red Creek, Wythe county, Virginia, was received as a vacancy, and was supplied, more or less, till the 10th of June, 1807, when it was turned over to the First Presbytery of the Carolinas. But it was too far away from any Associate Reformed centre to feel much warmth or receive much care, and has consequently long since ceased to exist, or passed to some other connection.

During the year 1803–4, several small vacancies in Virginia were recognized by Presbytery, and supplied according to its ability. One was in Rockingham county, another in Rock-

4

bridge county, another at the head of Smith river, and another
at Dry river. They were all feeble, and so situated that they
could not be conveniently grouped with other churches into
pastoral charges, and the Presbytery had not the men and
means with which to cultivate them vigorously, so they soon
dropped off and disappeared.

There was one other cluster of churches in the extreme corner of Virginia, in Washington county, in and around Abbingdon. They were known as Abbingdon, Beaver Creek, Silver
Spring, Rock Spring, Glade Spring, and the Middle Forks of
the Holston. They were regarded by Presbytery as one United
church, and whether they had but one organization, or several,
or how many, is not now known. It is probable that they
were formed during the last few years of the last century, and
that James Harper, Sr., who was received by Presbytery, December 25, 1799, from the Associate Presbytery of Derry, Ireland, first ministered to them. He died September 15, 1802,
and was succeeded by his son, James Harper, Jr., who was received by Presbytery, October 30, 1800, from the Associate
Presbytery of Derry, Ireland, and commenced to supply them
in the year 1802, and accepted, October 24, 1803, a call to become their pastor. The General Synod, in 1805, transferred
Mr. Harper and these churches to the Presbytery of Kentucky,
in the Synod of Scioto. As that Presbytery was distracted and
unhappy in all its history, making everything to wither that came
under its rule, so these churches soon passed from its roll, but not
from existence it is fondly hoped. Washington county, Virginia, is the centre of the Abbingdon Presbytery of the Southern
Presbyterian Church, and it is very probable that under her care,
these churches, or others which may have sprung from their
ashes, are still yielding fruit to the honor of our covenant God.
And thus it doubtless is with many or all of the churches
which the Big Spring Presbytery, or its predecessor, planted
and nourished amid the mountains of Virginia. They were
not crowded out by the influx of strangers of another creed
and nationality, but under the changing circumstances of our
progressive country, they were brought under new influences,
and entered into new connections where they not only wor-

shiped the God of their fathers, but did so with greater zeal and with more abundant fruits.

CUMBERLAND COUNTY.

In November, 1783, Rev. John Jamieson, of the Burgher Synod of Scotland, arrived in this country, and at once connected himself with the Associate Reformed church. After missionating nearly a year, he was installed, on the 22d of September, 1784, as pastor of the Big Spring congregation. This congregation included the Meanses, the Bards, the Kyles, and other families which lived in or near to Shippensburg; and for their accommodation Mr. Jamieson preached regularly, during his whole pastorate, a certain part of his time in Shippensburg. There was, however, no organization there: it was merely a preaching station of the Big Spring congregation, with which the members there were still connected. A strong dissatisfaction with Mr. Jamieson gradually grew up in his charge, partly because of some erroneous teaching and partly because of his jealous, fault-finding spirit, which made his manner somewhat imperious and repulsive. He was also constantly in trouble with his brethren in the Synod, and ceased to attend their meetings. For this neglect Synod, in 1790, directed his Presbytery to deal with him. The meeting in 1791 he attended, but in his published account of his subsequent trial, he tells us that he was so disgusted that he resolved to terminate his connection with the body. This threat he did not carry out, but in the Spring of 1792 he resigned his charge of Big Spring, and after spending a year in the Kentucky Presbytery, was installed, on the 11th of October, 1793, in the pastorate of Hannastown and connections, in Westmoreland county. Here he soon got into trouble, and after a series of trials in Presbytery and Synod, was finally deposed and excommunicated by Synod at its meeting in 1797, for false and injurious abuse of the Synod and some of its members, and for error in doctrine in reference to faith and the offer of the gospel to the reprobate. He was never restored, and some three years afterward he drifted westward into Ohio.

Mr. Jamieson was a man of decided abilities and of some

theological attainments; so that his Presbytery placed their theological students under his care, and Alexander Porter, Alexander McCoy and David Proudfit pursued their studies with him. He was undoubtedly a hyper-Calvinist, and leaned somewhat towards fatalism and antinomianism; but his greatest fault was his temper. Jealous and suspicious, and an ultra-conservative, he looked upon everything in this country, civil and ecclesiastical, as going to ruin; he could see nothing good or lovely outside of Scotch attainments in Church and State; and in politics as well as religion he was very successful in making himself unhappy.

In 1793 the church of Big Spring gave a call to the Rev. John Craig, who had just arrived from Ireland. This call was accepted, and he entered upon his labors. In the spring of 1794, Mr. T. Smith came as commissioner of Presbytery to install him, and found him dead, so that he was buried on the very day he was to have been installed. He was about fifty years old, and left a widow and three children; his only son, Abraham, became a minister, and long preached in the Associate Reformed church west of the mountains. A number of his descendants are now members and office holders in the United Presbyterian church.

In the summer of 1795, a call was given to a Mr. Kennedy, which was not accepted. Of this Mr. Kennedy the writer knows nothing.

About this time the congregation removed their old log meeting house and erected a new stone one upon the same site, more in harmony with the improved taste of the times. Its little windows and high, straight-backed, square pews, still remembered by a few, would look strange in our days. Churches have made greater advances in the matter of architecture, within the last hundred years than have dwelling houses.

In August, 1798, Big Spring resolved to call the Rev. James McConnell, just arrived from Ireland, but the cluster in Shippensburg refused to join in the call. This produced ill-feelings, and Big Spring, at a congregational meeting, September 1, 1798, unanimously resolved "to supplicate the Presbytery for a formal separation from Shippensburg." Their prayer was granted, and during the autumn of 1798, or most probably the spring of 1799, Mr. McConnell was installed as pastor of Big Spring.

As a preacher, Mr. McConnell was neither profound nor suggestive. His style was erratic, and he was disposed to confuse his hearers by the introduction of irrelevant matter. As a pastor he was active and diligent, and reasonably successful. His warm-hearted, convivial Irish temperament brought him sometimes into trouble, and twice they had to be adjudicated in Presbytery. On the 6th of November, 1809, he resigned, and a year afterward was transferred to the Presbytery of Monongahela, where he settled in Deer Creek and Puckety, and died March 3, 1848, at an advanced age.

After Mr. McConnell's departure, difficulties sprung up in the session, which threatened serious trouble. Some of its members had lost the confidence of a majority of the congregation, and to remedy matters, the whole session proposed to resign, so that the congregation might elect a new one. Not knowing how to do this, they asked permission and direction from the Presbytery, which were duly given. The peace offering was made, and the desired result was secured.

On the 20th of December, 1811, the congregation resolved to tender a call to the Rev. John M. Duncan; but when he was notified of this, he discourged the movement, and it never went to Presbytery, and he settled in Baltimore. In November, 1813, a call was given to Rev. John McFarland of the Presbytery of Kentucky, which was declined, and he settled in Chillicothe, Ohio. In 1819, an effort was made to secure the Rev. George Junkin, which, after some negotiation, failed. During the spring of 1822, a call was given to Joseph McCarrell, a native of Shippensburg, but this too was declined, and he settled in Newburg, New York.

Although Shippensburg was not incorporated as a borough till January, 1819, yet it is the oldest village west of the Susquehanna, excepting York. In June, 1730, Richard Morrow, John Culbertson, Alexander Caskey, Alexander Steen, John McCall, Hugh Rippey, John Strain, and four others, with their families settled here, and they were all Irish Presbyterians.

In 1733, "there were eighteen cabins in the town." In 1737, Edward Shippen of Philadelphia, father-in-law of Benedict Arnold, purchased of the Penns a large tract of land embracing the present town and much of the surrounding country, and the place took its name after him. At Middle Spring, three miles north of this, and midway between Big Spring and Rocky Spring, a preaching station was early established, and about 1740, a Presbyterian church was organized there. The Presbyterians of Shippensburg and vicinity belonged to this church; but Mr. Shippen and his agents, and the government employees at Forts Morris and Franklin located at Shippensburg, were Episcopalians, and an effort was made to establish an Episcopal church. This scheme, however, never promised to be successful, and when the agents and officers were withdrawn, it was wholly abandoned. The settlers had felt the iron hand of prelacy too sorely in Ireland to come readily to its embrace in this country. For fifty years there was no stated Presbyterian preaching in Shippensburg; the Synod of Ulster Irish went as best they could to Middle Spring, and the Seceder Irish to Big Spring. During the eight or nine years of Mr. Rodgers' pastorate, it is well nigh certain that he preached occasionally in Shippensburg, in passing through it almost every week between Big Spring and the Conecocheagues. But when Mr. Jamieson took charge of Big Spring this was recognized as a regular preaching station in his congregation, and he held services here about once a month, during his entire pastorate.

The lot numbered 216 on the village plot, was, June 2d, 1794, deeded by the Shippen brothers to the Associate Reformed church, and a stone meeting house was erected on it about the year 1797, which was subsequently enlarged, and still remains. It is impossible now to tell when the church was regularly and canonically organized, for it had a kind of half organization for years, but was still subordinate to or rather a constituent part of the congregation of Big Spring.

When the Shippensburgers refused to ratify Big Spring's election of Mr. McConnell, the congregation of Big Spring had a public meeting on the 1st of September, 1798, " To take

under consideration the distressed situation of the congregation, occasioned by the disorderly behavior of the community
of Shippensburg." The question was asked, "Can we remain
in connection with the community of Shippensburg? &c.," and
they resolved "to supplicate the Presbytery for a formal separation from Shippensburg." In all these proceedings towards
a separation, they never speak of the church or congregation
of Shippensburg, but always of the *community* of Shippensburg. From this, and other incidental circumstances, it might
be inferred that a regular and full organization did not take
place till after this separation. The probabilities are that
such is the fact, and the Presbytery, in October, 1798, directed
that it should be immediately and formally organized, and
united in a pastoral charge with Chambersburg, which was at
this time made vacant by the resignation of Matthew Lind.
In 1799, it first appeared on the roll of Presbytery, and was
doubtless organized during the spring of that year.

It is a matter of record, that in May, 1805, John Means,
William Bard and James Means were ordained and installed as
ruling elders, but there were elders previous to this. We
know that Matthew Kyle, who resided midway between Newville and Shippensburg, attended at the latter place during the
entire pastorate of Mr. Walker, and that he officiated as an
elder during all that time, and the presumption is, that he was
ordained and installed at the organization of the church.
There is a bare possibility that Marshall Means and John
Mitchell were associated with him, but of this there is no certainty. The four elders mentioned lived till after the congregation passed into the Presbyterian Church, and no additions
were made.

During the autumn of 1798, or early spring of '99, James
Walker was received by the First Presbytery of Pennsylvania,
as a probationer from the Associate Presbytery of Down, Ireland, and on the 4th of September, 1799, he was ordained and
installed as pastor of the congregation of Shippensburg and
Chambersburg. He resided in Shippensburg, and gave half of
his time to each place. On the 8th of August, 1820, he resigned, received a certificate of dismission from the Presbytery,

and removed to the west. Mr. Walker was clerk of the Presbytery of Big Spring from its organization till his removal, and was very punctual in his duties as a presbyter. He was a large, heavy-set man, rather pompous in his manners, although genial in spirit. He always carried a cane, and never preached without gloves, and had the reputation of being a good preacher.

In March, 1821, Shippensburg and Chambersburg gave a call to the Rev. Robert McCartee, which was declined. On the 23d of October, 1821, Thomas M. Strong was ordained and installed over these two churches. Immediately after Mr. Strong's settlement, a union was formed between his congregation in Shippensburg and the members of the Presbyterian church at Middle Spring, who resided in or near the village. By this means, quite an accession was made to the church of very excellent families, and the only wonder was, that something of this kind had not been done many years before, for the difficulties in the way were but very few, as the old Psalms were as dearly cherished in Middle Spring as in Shippensburg, and remained in both places as the psalmody of the church until but a few years ago. The only possible reason for remaining apart was a difference upon the subject of communion, and as Mr. Strong had been a student of Dr. Mason, and sympathized with his views, this reason ceased to operate.

The congregation of Big Spring had some outlying families in and around Carlisle, and westward along the Walnut Bottom road, which did not go into the union of 1782. They sympathized with the residuary party in the old Presbytery, and waited hopefully for the future. About 1789, the Presbytery had been so strengthened by the arival of three or four ministers from Scotland, that it was able to look after these families, and began to send them supplies. In 1796, a lot on West street, in Carlisle, was conveyed by the Penns, in consideration of six pounds, to William Blair, William Moore, John Smith and John McCoy, as trustees of the "Associate Presbyterian congregation, adhering to the subordination of the Associate Presbytery of Pennsylvania, of which the Rev. William Marshall and James Clarkson were then members." It is believed that the church was not regularly organized by Presbytery till 1798, and that this action was taken in anticipation of such event A stone building was erected in 1802, and during the same year Rev. Francis Pringle, who came from Ireland in 1799, was installed as pastor. The Woodburns, the Rosses, the Moores, and a number more of the most substantial and leading families of the congregation lived at a considerable distance in the country, and for their convenience it was deemed expedient to provide a preaching place in the country where public services could be occasionally held. Mr. Moore, of Dickinson township, donated an acre from the corner of his farm, about six miles from Carlisle, as a site for a meeting-house and graveyard, and here, in 1809 or 1810, a stone church was built. There was no separate organizations in any sense; it was a mere preaching station, and the sacrament of the Supper was probably never administered in the house; the communion services were always observed in Carlisle by the entire congregation. In addition to his pastoral labors, Mr. Pringle did considerable missionary work in the small vacancies at Mercersburg, and in Huntingdon county.

ADAMS COUNTY.

In the minutes of the Associate Reformed Synod, which met in Philadelphia in November, 1783, it is recorded that "Mr. Murray, minister at Marsh Creek, in name of his congregation, gave in a verbal petition, requesting the advice of Synod in their case. Agreed that Mr. Murray, in consideration of his infirm state of health, be at liberty to give up his pastoral charge of that congregation, continuing, however, to exercise the office of the ministry among them, as he shall find ability; and that the Synod will contribute what they are able towards his comfortable support, and that the Moderator write a pressing letter to said congregation on this head."

Mr. Murray died during the following year, in the prime of manhood. We can find but few memorials of him, but those few present him in a favorable way. It is believed that he came from Scotland in 1773, in company with Mr. Logan; that he was thoroughly educated, and was held in esteem by his parishioners and his fellow-presbyters.

Indeed, it is worthy of note, that all the ministers sent out in those early days, were men of fine education and good standing at home. They came, not because they could not find a charge in their native land, but because they were sent by Synod as suitable men to found the Church in this new and distant country.

In the autumn of 1785, or spring of 1786, Mr. Dobbin, of Rock Creek, was called and installed for half his time in Marsh Creek, and thus he continued to divide his time to the end of his ministry. These two congregations have ever since remained associated in the same pastoral charge.

The Rock Creek congregation built their first house for worship of logs, near the stream which gave it its name, and situated about one mile northeast of where Gettysburg now stands. Here they worshiped till 1805, when a new house was erected in the village of Gettysburg, which was now starting up. This was the first church built by any denomination in the village. It was a substantial structure of brick, of good size, finished in the old style, with high-backed pews, brick paved aisles, high pulpit, and huge sounding board. It has since been modernized, and promises to serve the congregation comfortably for many years to come. In 1808, they were incorporated by an act of the Legislature as " The Associate Reformed Congregation of Gettysburg."

On the 15th of April, 1807, the Synod of Pennsylvania transferred Mr. Dobbin and his charge from the Presbytery of Philadelphia to the Presbytery of Big Spring, for the purpose of strengthening the latter Presbytery. In the autumn of 1809, after Mr. Dobbin's death, the congregations were returned to their original connection.

On the 20th of October, 1808, Mr. Dobbin preached while laboring under a severe cold, which resulted in a hemorrhage of the lungs, and this soon settled into a rapid consumption, from which he died on the 1st of June, 1809, in the 67th year of his age, and was buried in the Marsh Creek graveyard, where he had garnered two wives and several children.

Mr. Dobbin was the son of a pious sailor, and was born in Londonderry, Ireland, in 1742; was thoroughly educated at Glasgow University, and was licensed and immediately afterwards ordained by the Reformed Presbytery of Scotland, as a missionary to the New World. He landed at New Castle, Delaware, about the middle of December, 1773, and during the summer of 1774 was installed at Rock Creek, where he continued till his death. He took a very active part in accomplishing the union of 1782, and always held a prominent and honored position in the Associate Reformed Church. He was an accomplished linguist, especially in Hebrew, and established the first Classical School west of the Susquehanna, and more than sixty of his pupils became professional men, and not less than twenty-five of them ministers of the gospel. Before the establishment of the Theological Seminary in New York, he had trained eight of our early ministers in Hebrew and Theology. As a presbyter, and as a pastor, he was active, diligent and laborious; as a preacher, he was both interesting and instructive, and dwelt much and lovingly upon the doctrines of the atonement, the offices of Christ, and the work of the Mediator. In disposition, he was very cheerful and agreeable, and in social intercourse, was much enjoyed because of his wit and playfulness. Dr. McJimsey, who was reared under his ministry, and largely educated classically and theologically by him, testified of him, that he possessed " an uncommon combination of ministerial gifts and graces, of prudence, of meekness, of faithfulness in the discharge of public duty, of the love of peace, and pleasantness of temper."

In 1812, John M. Duncan received a call as successor to Mr. Dobbin, which he declined; and in the spring of 1814, Charles G. McLean was ordained and installed as pastor of the churches in Gettysburg and at "the Hill," and so remained for nearly thirty years.

YORK COUNTY.

After the union of 1782, the church at Muddy Creek or Guinston, although denominationally isolated from the surrounding churches, enjoyed peace and harmony within itself, and prospered in all its material and spiritual interests. In accordance with the directions of the Associate Presbytery of Pennsylvania. one hundred and twenty-one of the members of this congregation engaged, in October, 1793, in a public renewal of their Covenant engagements. This it is believed was the first time and the only time that this church engaged publicly and formally in this work. Shortly after the commencement of the present century, Mr. Clarkson's health began to fail, and in May, 1805, he applied to Synod for a supply for his pulpit, which was granted, although he continued to act as moderator of session, until he resigned his charge, in March, 1808. The congregation continued to minister to his support until his death, which occurred on the 30th of October, 1811, when he had entered upon the seventy-fourth year of his age.

Mr. Miller describes Mr. Clarkson as "a systematic and doctrinal preacher generally. Though he could not be called an eloquent speaker, yet he was an interesting preacher. He had an impressive earnestness in his manner, well calculated to draw attention. His enunciation was clear, manly and distinct; and though he sometimes hesitated, he would frequently speak with fluency. All his talents were of the useful, rather than of the brilliant kind. As a man he was cheerful and affable; at the same time he possessed a native dignity, of which he could not easily divest himself, undeviatingly adhering to whatever he conceived to be right, regardless of consequences."

Guinston made many efforts before they were successful in getting a successor to Mr. Clarkson. On the 17th of June, 1808, they gave a call to the Rev. Robert Bruce, which was declined; in 1810, they called the Rev. John Mushet, but he declined; in 1814, they made a determined effort to get Alexander McClelland for their pastor, and offered him an installation present of more than a hundred dollars, but they were still unsuccessful; in 1816, they called Alexander Wilson, and he too declined their call. Finally, on the 20th of August, 1818, Alexander Gordon was ordained and installed as their pastor. .

Having received their new minister, the congregation exhibited new energy and activity, and formed new plans for the

more thorough cultivation of their field. In 1819, they formed
a local Bible Society auxiliary to the American Bible Society,
and established two Sabbath Schools embracing more than
sixty members. In 1821, a portion of the Associate Reformed
congregation in Lower Chanceford, became very much dissatisfied with the course of the Philadelphia Presbytery, to which
they belonged, in reference to the proposed union with the
Presbyterian Church, and during that and the succeeding year
transferred their membership to the Guinston church, without
determining whether the arrangement should be permanent,
or only temporary, according to the results of the union efforts.

In reference to the origin of the church of Hopewell there
are no records, and but fragmentary traditions. The probabilities are that its first families were connected with the Muddy
Creek or Guinston congregation, and separated themselves
therefrom, when Mr. Clarkson and the great body of his charge
declined going into the union. This led them to associate
themselves with their more distant neighbors in Lower Chanceford, and for twenty years Hopewell was in reality, if not in
form, an out-lying preaching station of that church, and for
half a century more, connected with it in a pastoral charge.

The first Presbytery of Pennsylvania reported to Synod at
its meeting in New York, October 21st, 1802, that "a Mr.
Charles Campbell, who came into this country under a sentence
of suspension from the holy ministry, by the Associate Presbytery of Derry, in Ireland, but fully purged of scandal, and restored to the communion of the church, has been admitted to
preach the gospel under the care of Presbytery, in order to
make trial of his humble and pious deportment previous to his
restoration to the ministerial office; and as far as is known has
given general satisfaction, both in his public ministrations and
private deportment." Synod was by no means pleased with
this action, and "Resolved, That the conduct of the First Presbytery of Pennsylvania, in restoring Mr. Campbell to preach the
gospel, was incautious and precipitate; that they and the other
Presbyteries under the inspection of this Synod, be and they
hereby are required to exercise the utmost caution in the admission of ministers from other countries without satisfactory

testimonials." It was further " *Resolved*, That the case of Mr.
Campbell (that is, his restoration to the ministry) be referred
to the Synod of Pennsylvania; and that they defer any deci-
sion thereon until official information be received from the Associate Presbytery of Derry, in Ireland, by which he was suspended." It was also "Ordered, That the First Presbytery of
Pennsylvania write, without delay, to the Associate Presbytery of Derry, in Ireland, requesting such information." The
minutes of the Synod of Pennsylvania are lost, but it is believed that Mr. Campbell was restored to the ministry, by the
Synod at its first meeting, held May 25th, 1803, at Marsh
Creek. The probabilities are that Mr. Campbell came to this
country in the summer or autumn of 1801, and having been
granted the privilege by Presbytery of preaching as a probationer for restoration to the ministry, he began, in November
of that year, to serve Lower Chanceford and Hopewell as stated
supply. Two-thirds of his time to the former, and one-third
to the latter, which was organized about 1801, and most likely
in view of this arrangement.

These churches gave Mr. Campbell a call to become their
pastor, and he accepted it, but whether his installation ever
took place, the writer is not able to determine, most probably
it did in the latter part of 1803, for Mr. Campbell, soon after
this, on the 7th of April, 1804, died, in the thirty-sixth year of
his age. He was born in Stewardstown, in county of Tyrone,
Ireland; was educated under Brown of Haddington; was
licensed before he was twenty-one years of age, and preached
in the county of Londonderry. His short career in this country
was very quiet and uneventful, but he left a pleasant memory
both as a man and as a preacher.

The Rev. Josiah Wilson, of Armagh, Ireland, and a student
of Brown of Haddington, was installed, January 1, 1808, as
pastor of Lower Chanceford and Hopewell; but his pastorate
was also short, for he died in September, 1812. Having been
trained in medicine, he was to a certain extent the physician as
well as spiritual guide of his flock. He was held in high esti-
mation for his learning and consistent piety.

In 1806, these congregations had given a call to the Rev.

Thomas Smith of Tuscarora, which was declined: and in 1818, they called Mr. Isaiah Niblock, but without success, and a long vacancy was then experienced.

PERRY AND JUNIATA COUNTIES.

When Mr. Logan began to preach in Fermanagh in 1777, the boundaries of his congregation were not definitely fixed in any direction; and he did a considerable amount of missionary work for many miles around. Immediately south of the Juniata river and the Tuscarora mountain is the valley of Racoon Creek, which was early settled by Irish, and often visited by Mr. Logan. Towards the end of the last century a small congregation was organized here, and recognized as a part of Mr. Logan's pastoral charge without any of the formalities of a call or installation. This congregation embraced not only the lower part of Racoon Valley, but stretched across the river, and included the country around what is now Millerstown. When Fermanagh was joined to Tuscarora, Mr. Smith did not assume the pastoral care of Millerstown, as this congregation was now called, and for three or four years it was dependent upon supplies from Presbytery. In 1809, it was assigned by Presbytery to Mr. Smith, as a part of his charge, and to receive one-fifth of his time. This arrangement continued only a year, although Mr. Smith for ten years afterwards preached there occasionally as he could make it convenient. The result of this isolation and irregular supply was, that those on the north side of the river became assimilated with the Thompsontown end of the Fermanagh congregation, and those in Racoon Valley became lost to the Associate Reformed Church.

About 1802 or '3, Mr. Logan's health became so feeble that he was unable to ride to the church, but as his dwelling house was large he had the congregation gathered there, and he continued to preach to them every Sabbath. On the 19th of May, 1805, he preached in his house as usual and with his usual ability in the morning, and during the interval of worship he retired to his study to rest, before commencing the afternoon services. During that half hour's rest, without any special premonition, he suddenly died, literally falling with his armor on. He left no children, and his widow moved to Carlisle where she soon died. He was much respected for his learning and piety both in his congregation and in the community. The following inscription on his tombstone gives a fair epitome of his life and character:

"Interred
is the dust of the
Rev. William Logan.
Scotland
Is the place of his birth and education.
The sacred ministry his choice.
He was born in the year 1743.
Arrived in America 1773.
Died suddenly on Sabbath, May 19, 1805, in the
63d year of his age after preaching that forenoon.
For 28 years, with diligence and fidelity, he
discharged the duty of his office to his flock in
Fermanagh and Racoon Valley.
Prudence, Piety, Moderation, Good Sense, and
Sound Patriotism were some of his
Characteristics.
A faithful husband and a steady friend."

Tuscarora valley was settled as early as 1745, and by the same class of immigrants that first peopled all these valleys west of the Susquehanna. They sought and received supply of preaching from the Associate Presbytery of Pennsylvania as soon as that Presbytery had any supply to send, but a church, it is believed, was not formally organized till about 1801, or the year in which the Rev. T. Smith was installed as its pastor by the First Associate Reformed Presbytery of Pennsylvania.

Thomas Dobbs, James Innis, William Hart and Robert Black constituted its first board of ruling elders. The probabilities are that Mr. Smith gave only one-half of his time to Tuscarora, for we have evidence that he spent much of his time in preaching in different places beyond the limits of that congregation, particularly in Hare's valley, and in Path valley, and in the valley of Kishacoquillas. When Fermanagh became vacant by the death of Mr. Logan, it applied to Presbytery to be united to Tuscarora in one pastoral charge, under the care of Mr. Smith. After considerable delay and negotiation, it was finally arranged by Presbytery in 1808, that Mr. Smith should preach two-fifths of his time in Tuscarora, two-fifths in Fermanagh, and one-fifth in Kishacoquillas. In 1809, the last place was dropped, and Millerstown was substituted. But in 1810, this place was also dropped, and Mr. Smith, during the remainder of his life, divided his time equally between Tuscarora and Fermanagh, and always resided in the former place. Mr. Smith was particularly opposed to the attempted union of 1822. He spoke against it, and voted against it in the General Synod. He raised the point of order that the plan was not adopted because it did not receive the affirmative vote of a majority of the members present, and he prepared and offered the protest of those who voted in the negative.

Path Valley was so called because the great Indian trail or path from the Susquehanna to the Ohio passed through it. The village of Concord is situated in this valley in the extreme northern point of Franklin county. This section of country was first visited by Mr. Smith, and after a little culture, it was recognized as a preaching station in 1807, and supplied by the Big Spring Presbytery. In 1815, it was organized as a church, and in December, of the same year, gave a call to the Rev. James Brown. The Presbytery was not clear as to duty in the matter of receiving Mr. Brown and sustaining this call, inasmuch as Mr. Brown had been ordained by the Evangelical Association of Ireland, and there were some doubts as to the validity of such an ordination. The question of validity was referred to the General Synod, and finally decided in Mr. Brown's favor, and in June, 1817, he was installed at Concord. This settlement was made with the understanding that the cluster of families of Associate Reformed preferences, which resided in the neighborhood of Fannetsburg, and those in the region of Shirleysburg, would contribute to Mr. Brown's support, and receive a proportionate amount of preaching. This expectation was not realized, and Concord soon found itself unable to support its pastor. In about two years, Mr. Brown resigned, and Concord remained vacant for the next ten years.

Mr. Brown was born in county of Tyrone, in Ireland, and

5

received a collegiate, a theological, and medical education in
the University of Edinburg, Scotland. He was ordained by
the Evangelical Association of Ireland, and came with his
family to this country in 1810, and preached for several years
as stated supply in Perry county. After leaving Concord he
spent two or three years at Timber Ridge and Old Providence,
in Virginia, and then went to western Pennsylvania. In 1829,
he settled in Pittsburgh as a practicing physician, and 1839, removed to Bridgewater, Pa., where he remained till his death,
which occurred on the 20th of December, 1854, in the sixty-
fifth year of his age, and in the full faith of his Saviour's love.

HUNTINGDON COUNTY.

Our present sources of information would indicate, that the
valleys of Huntingdon county were first visited by Associate
ministers during the last four years of the last century, and
that some time in the year 1800, the Rev. F. Pringle organized
a church in the county seat, and ordained and installed as ruling elders, John Carman, John Smart, John Brown, Thomas
Johnston, James Irwin, Joseph Henderson, Alexander McConnell, and Joseph Corbin. This organization was not confined
to the town of Huntingdon, but included a number of small
settlements located several miles in different directions in the
surrounding country. Their first effort towards securing a
pastor, was the giving of a call, in August 1808, to the Rev.
Robert Bruce, who had arrived in the year 1806, from Scotland.
Failing in this they were dependent upon Presbyterial supply till
the 28th of November, 1811, when the Rev. Thomas Smith, a
native of Scotland, was installed as their first pastor. While
there was but one organization, and one bench of elders, yet
his charge was composed of three branches, to each of which,
for one hundred dollars per year, he gave the one-third of his
time. These were located in Huntingdon, in Petersburg, and
in Woodcock Valley. There were also out stations which he
frequently visited, in Sinking Valley, at Drake's Ferry, and at
Newton Hamilton. In the process of time and in consequence
of the constant shifting of the population, all these branches
and out stations, except Huntingdon, were dropped, and the

Secession cause soon died out. But the valley of Stone Creek seemed to have some special attraction to the families of Seceder antecedents or proclivities, for they gathered more and more into it, and especially into its upper part. Mr. Smith, like a good shepherd followed the flock and formed a station up the valley at Manor Hill, which flourished for a season, even after Huntingdon had commenced to decrease. In 1808, the congregation built in Huntingdon, a meeting house of logs, and furnished it with only rough seats. It was not entirely finished till 1822, and as it had no arrangement for heating, services in cold weather were still held in the court house up to that time. This was the first church building erected by any denomination in Huntingdon, and rude as it was, it served the congregation as long as it was needed. In 1817 a house similar in structure and equally comfortless was provided at Manor Hill; it too served its day and the demands of its location.

All the Churches in this country soon realized that they must not depend upon the Old Country for their supply of ministers. Hence each one early made some provision for their home education. Dr. Tennent began in 1726 to train theological students in his college at Neshaminy. Dr. Nisbet, of Carlisle, and other Presbyterian ministers did the same. The Reformed Dutch church sent her students to Dr. Livingstone. Before the union of 1782 the Associate Presbytery sent hers to Mr. Smith of Octorara. Immediately after the union of 1782 Mr. Dobbin undertook the instruction of Associate Reformed students. In 1793 the Second Associate Reformed Presbytery of Pennsylvania sent its candidates for the ministry to John Jamieson. In 1794 the Associate Presbytery of Pensylvania consigned its students to the care of Dr. John Anderson. But in all these instances the course of instruction was very imperfect, for it consisted mainly in a course of lectures on Systematic Theology and a little Hebrew. About the beginning of this century, Dr. Mason insisted upon a fuller course of instruction and a larger corps of teachers. This Presbytery entered heartily into the scheme, and Messrs. Dobbin and Young were members of the committee of the Synod of 1801, which reported in its favor, and started the enterprise. And when the

Seminary was opened in the autumn of 1805, with a class of eight students, the Presbytery of Big Spring supplied four of those eight, in the persons of John Lind, George Buchanan, George Stewart and John X. Clark.

CHAPTER III.

THE UNION OF 1822.

HE General Synod run smoothly and the Church prospered under it till the year 1811, when controversies more or less bitter and personal, touching the questions of psalmody and communion began to mix up with its proceedings, and were never absent from its subsequent meetings. Several unpleasant cases of discipline occurred at this time, which destroyed the Presbytery of Kentucky, and greatly agitated the entire Church. These things with others of a more local and personal character, injured the unity of purpose and the harmony of feelings in the body, and brought in jealousy and distrust and divided counsels, and as a natural consequence every interest of the church began to languish. In 1817 the Synod of Scioto asked that the General Synod should meet, occasionally at least, in a more western and central place than Philadelphia, where it now always met, that the Synods of Scioto and the Carolinas might be better represented in its proceedings; or, if this could not be granted, that the church should be divided into two or more separate and independent Synods. Both of these requests were refused. The result of all these things combined was that the Synod of Scioto, at its meeting at Rush Creek, Ohio, on the 27th of April, 1820, constituted itself into an independent Synod, under the title of the Associate Reformed Synod of the West.

In 1821, the Synod of the Carolinas petitioned the General Synod for a separate and independent organization; which was granted, and it constituted itself at its next meeting, as the Associate Reformed Synod of the South. This left under the supervision of the General Synod, only the two Synods of Pennsylvania and New York.

At the meeting of the General Synod at Philadelphia, in May, 1821, an overture was received from the General Assembly of the Presbyterian church, then and there in session, proposing an organic union of the two churches. Committees were appointed by both bodies to conduct the negotiations; and the following plan was agreed upon as a basis of union, viz: That the "different Presbyteries of the Associate Reformed church should either retain their separate organization, or be amalgamated with those of the General Assembly, at their own choice:" That "the Theological Seminary at Princeton, under the care of the General Assembly, and the Theological Seminary of the Associate Reformed church should be consolidated:" And that "the Theological Library, and funds belonging to the Associate Reformed church, shall be transferred, and belong to the Seminary at Princeton." This plan was overtured to its Presbyteries by the General Synod, but not by the General Assembly.

The General Synod met in Philadelphia on the 15th of May, 1822. Of the *twenty-two* delegates commissioned, only *sixteen* attended. The Presbytery of Washington was entirely unrepresented; and there was one absent from the Presbytery of Saratoga, and one from the Presbytery of Big Spring. The subject of union with the Presbyterian church was taken up, and the Presbyteries of Washington and Saratoga reported unanimously against the union; Big Spring against with a small minority favorable; and the Presbyteries of New York and Philadelphia in favor of the union with a small minority in each against it. Notwithstanding this presbyterial rejection, the subject was discussed at length for the greater part of four days, when on Tuesday, the 21st of May, it was resolved "That this Synod approve, and hereby do ratify the plan of union between the General Assembly of the Presbyterian Church and the Associate Reformed Church, proposed by commissioners from said churches." The vote upon this resolution was, ayes, 7; noes, 5; silent, 4; viz:

YEAS.

Rev. James Laurie, D. D.,	of the Presbytery of Philadelphia.
Rev. Ebenezer Dickey, D. D.,	" " "
Rev. John M. Duncan,	" " "
Elder Joseph Nourse,	" " "

Elder James Martin,   of the Presbytery of Philadelphia.
Elder Robert Patterson,   "   "   "
Elder John Forsyth, of Murray street church, Presbytery of New York.

NAYS.

Rev. Robert Forrest, '   of the Presbytery of Saratoga.
Rev. James Otterson,   "   "   "
Elder Samuel Lefferts,   "   "   "
Rev. Thomas Smith,   "   "   Big Spring
Elder James McCulloch,   "   "   "

SILENT.

Rev. William W. Phillips.   of the Presbyter of New York.
Rev. Robert B. E. McLeod,   "   "   "
Elder Robert Blake,   "   "   "
Rev. John Lind,   "   "   Big Spring.

Objection was made that seven yeas did not consitute a majority of the Synod and that the resolution was not adopted. Dr. Laurie, the moderator, decided that silent votes were to be reckoned with the majority, and that the resolution was carried. Those who voted in the negative protested against this action, because it was against the voice of the church, as a majority of its congregations and ministers and presbyteries were opposed to the union; and because it "was effected by the delegates from the Presbytery of Philadelphia alone, only one member from the remaining four Presbyteries voting in its favor."

It was known that at least *five* of the six absent delegates were opposed to the union; and giving to the union all that were silent or doubtful, the popular vote of the church would have been *fourteen* ministers and *fifteen* churches for the union; and *eighteen* ministers and *nineteen* churches against it.

The General Assembly was at once advised of the adoption of the plan of union and a union thanksgiving was held next day in the Assembly's house, a psalm and a hymn were sung, two prayers were offered, and the delegates to the General Synod were invited to take their seats forthwith in the Assembly as constituent members. On the 23d of May, Reverends R. B. E. McLeod and J. M. Duncan, and Elders J. Nourse and R. Patterson did take their seats in the Assembly, and it is stated in the minutes of the General Assembly that "The rest of the members of the Synod, having made arrangements to return home, were unable to attend the Assembly."

The General Synod, or the union portion of it, met again on Thursday morning, and adopted the draft of a pastoral letter to the churches in explanation and defence of their course, and directed the clerk of Synod, Mr. Arbuckle, to deposit all the minutes and documents of the General Synod with the session of the Spruce street congregation, "subject to the future disposal of the General Assembly of the Presbyterian Church." They then sung, not the usual 133d Psalm, but more fitting penitential 130th Psalm, and "finally adjourned." Thus perished the old General Synod after a somewhat troubled existence of only eighteen years; and with it perished the subordinate Synod of Pennsylvania. The Presbytery of Philadelphia, in accordance with the plan of union, went into the Presbyterian Church as a distinct presbyterial organization, and appeared for two years upon the roll of the General Assembly as the *Second* Presbytery of Philadelphia.

As this *Second* Presbytery and its queer offspring will meet us hereafter, it may be well to give their brief history here. The Second Presbytery was represented in the General Assembly of 1823, by Ebenezer Dickey, D. D., and in the Assembly of 1824 by Henry R. Wilson, and James Arbuckle. In the autumn of 1824 this Presbytery consisted of E. Dickey, J. M. Duncan, H. R. Wilson, C. G. McLean, and George Junkin, pastors; Joseph Wallace and David Kirkpatrick, without charge, and John Chambers, licentiate. Dr. Laurie had gone, in 1822, to the Presbytery of Baltimore, Dr. Gray died September 20, 1823, and T. G. McInnis of the 13th street church died August 26, 1824, and Mr. Arbuckle had accepted a call elsewhere. In the winter of 1824–5, this Presbytery voted certificates of transfer to all its members that they might join the Presbytery of their several localities. This they nearly all did. Mr. Duncan in the summer of 1824 had delivered a lecture before the directors and students of the Theological Seminary at Princeton, at their solicitation. He called his lecture "A Plea for Ministerial Liberty," and in it condemned in very strong language all creeds and confessions, and scouted the idea of church standards, declaring that they only crippled and circumscribed that liberty wherewith Christ makes his people free. When he presented his certificate to the Presbytery of Baltimore in the spring of 1825, he was unanimously rejected, because of the doctrines maintained in his discourse. He appealed to Synod but got no relief. Mr. McLean of Gettysburg, who sympathized with Mr. Duncan in his views, was either afraid or deemed it inexpedient to offer his certificate to the Presbytery of Carlisle; so he and Duncan and John Chambers and a Mr. Jewett organized, in the autumn of 1825, a Presbytery of their own, which they called "The Independent Presbytery." It was thoroughly independent, and at no point touched any other ecclesiastical organization, and as might have been expected it never warmed actively into life, and after a few years of feeble existence it passed away without even the formality of a final adjournment.

CHAPTER IV.

1822 TO 1858.

THE union of 1822 not only distracted but literally divided the Presbytery of Big Spring into three fragments. The Presbytery met at Shippensburg in August, 1822, and dissolved the pastorial relation between Mr. Strong and the churches of Shippensburg and Chambersburg, and dismissed him to the Long Island Classis of the Reformed Dutch Church. Dr. Strong was installed in the Dutch church of Flat Bush, in 1822, and remained its beloved and useful pastor until his death in 1861. He was a tall, fine-looking man, an excellent preacher, possessed a singularly well-balanced mind, and left a reputation particularly dear to his Church. For thirty-four years he was stated clerk of the General Synod of the Dutch Church, and so thoroughly versed was he in ecclesiastical matters that in the Synod his word was law. "And yet," says a friend who knew him well, "there never was a more modest and unassuming man." He left five sons, all of whom are now in the ministry.

Mr. Lind and his churches would not go into the General Assembly, neither would they go into the Synod of the West, so they remained independent and alone. Mr. Smith and the churches of Fermanagh, Tuscarora, Concord, Chambersburg and Big Spring put themselves under the care of the Monongahela Presbytery of the Synod of the West. Shippensburg joined the Second Presbytery of Philadelphia. Thus the Big Spring Presbytery ceased to exist, until it was re-organized in May, 1825, by the Synod of the West, with which it remained until that Synod was divided in 1839, and since the union of 1858, it has been subordinate to the United Presbyterian Synod of Pittsburgh.

Mr. Lind was in favor of a union with the Presbyterian Church, but was opposed to the precipitate and uncanonical

manner in which it was consummated. He was grieved with
the course of those with whom he sympathized, and declined
to go into the union; yet he would not transfer his relation
to the Synod of the West, so when the Big Spring Presbytery
went to pieces, he sought no connection, and thus dropped out
of all ecclesiastical association. His congregations were much
attached to him, and stood by him now, and were willing to
be governed by his future movements. And so they remained
for two years, and then Providence decided the question.
During the summer of 1824, Mr. Lind concluded that their
state of isolation was not good for either pastor or people, and
made arrangements to connect himself and his churches with
the Presbytery of Carlisle at its meeting in October. But on
Saturday, the 4th of September, he preached to his church in
Hagerstown, preparatory to the observance of the Lord's Supper on the next day. Before finishing the services, he was
seized with a severe chill, from which he suffered all night, and
Sabbath morning found him no better, but hearing that a
large congregation had assembled, he rose from his bed and
went to the church, and with great feebleness, but peculiar
unction, he simply dispensed the Supper. Before finishing
this brief service, he was taken with another chill, and was
unable to proceed, so he lifted his hand and said, " Beloved
brothers and sisters in Christ, as ye have received the Lord
Jesus, so walk in Him," and pronounced the apostolic bene-
diction. He returned to his bed and gradually sunk till the
20th of September, when he calmly died, in the forty-first year
of his age, and the eighteenth of his ministry.

Mr. Lind was in many respects a man of mark. He took
the honors of his class in college; he was informally offered
the professorship in the Theological Seminary as Dr. Mason's
successor; he was tendered the Presidency of Dickinson College; he had a call to the Murray Street church in New York,
and also to the First church in Pittsburg, but he declined them
all that he might remain with the people of his childhood and
of his manhood. He was tall and handsome in person, of fine
mental culture, and of very considerable pulpit power. But
his great characteristic, and the one which gave him the strong-

est hold upon the affections of his people and the community at large, was a peculiarly mild and amiable disposition ; a trait of character which he attributed not to nature, but to grace.

In April, 1825, the churches of Hagerstown and Green Castle joined the Presbytery of Carlisle of the Presbyterian Church, and in September of the same year, Matthew Lind Fullerton, grandson of Rev. Matthew Lind, was ordained and installed as their pastor. At this time Mr. Buchanan was pastor of the Presbyterian churches of Green Castle and Waynesborough, preaching alternate Sabbaths in each. There were now two Presbyterian churches in Green Castle, and the pastors arranged to preach on alternate Sabbaths, and the audience was composed of the people of both congregations.

As the doctrines and forms and Psalmody of both churches were the same, and as they now attended upon the same ministry, they soon became practically one church. In 1827 or '8, they formally united, and Mr. Buchanan gave to them all his time, and Mr. Fullerton confined his labors to Hagerstown. In 1830, the two old church buildings, the " White " and the " Red," were abandoned for a new one, larger and more centrally situated, and the " Old White " was taken down and moved two miles into the country, and re-built for a dwelling-house, and thus passed away the last trace and memorial of Dissenting Presbyterianism, which, as Reformed, as Associate, and as Associate Reformed, had existed on the East Conecocheague for seventy years.

Mr. Fullerton remained in Hagerstown till his death in 1833, and was succeeded by Richard Wynkoop, who, through controversies in Presbytery with Dr. Duffield, became involved in troubles in his own congregation, which resulted in a division, when he and a majority of the church, in 1838, united with the Associate Reformed Presbytery of New York. Four years afterwards, Mr. Wynkoop died, and for two years the church was supplied by the Presbyteries of New York and Big Spring. In the autumn of 1844, a call was given to the Rev. John F. McLaren, late of Geneva, N. Y., and he was installed as pastor April 23, 1845 ; but he remained only a few months, for in the autumn of that year the two divisions of the original congregations came together, and the united church put itself under the care of the Presbytery of Carlisle, and thus ended Associate Reformedism in Hagerstown.

While one congregation after another was passing away, it is a consolation to know that there was some compensation in the way of gathering. In 1794, Thomas Johnston, of the Associate church of Pequea, Lancaster county, settled in the neighborhood of Mercersburg, and connected himself with the little vacancy at Carlisle, the nearest Associate preaching station. Here he attended services as often as he could, and especially on communion occasions. Athough two or three families associated themselves with him, and his sons began to settle around him, yet the situation continued substantially thus till 1814, when the Associate Presbytery of Philadelphia recognized them as a mission station, and began to send them occasional supplies. Messrs. Pringle, Kendall, Scroggs, Blair, and others visited them, and they grew a little. When Mr. Lind resigned the West Conecocheague branch of his charge in 1817, the Rankins and several other families were not willing to join the Presbyterian Church, nor to stand aloof from all church relations, and had no prospect of re-building the Associate Reformed cause, so they united with this Associate nucleus, and this gave them strength and hope. They sought and obtained an organization in August, 1822, and about the first of September gave a call to Thomas B. Clarkson. This call he held under consideration, and supplied the pulpit till May 31, 1823, when he accepted it, and was installed on the 8th of the succeeding October. The Associate Reformed church in the Cove Valley, notwithstanding its utter destitution, still maintained its organization, and wisely concluded to unite with Mercersburg in this settlement, and thus connected themselves with the Associate Church, Mr. Clarkson assuring them that he could cover the differences between the two Churches with his thumb.

Mr. Clarkson's ministry was very successful, so that in 1826, he reported one hundred and eighty-four members in his two congregations. But his health became very feeble, so that after much waiting and hoping the pastoral relation was dissolved

in December, 1827. He remained in the community till his
death in 1836, and is still tenderly remembered. He is described
as "a man of fine personal appearance, and of remarkably
graceful and attractive manners. So much of natural vivacity
had he, and withal so much christian principle and feeling,
that it seemed as if no disease or trouble, nor even the near
approach of death, could have any effect upon his spirits."

On the 20th of May, 1828, Findley W. McNaughton, a
native of Argyle, New York, was ordained and installed as
pastor of Mercersburg and the Cove. Messrs. Clarkson, Francis
Pringle and Arch. Whyte officiated upon the occasion. The
Mercersburg branch now contained ninety-one members, and
had never owned a church edifice. They had worshiped a short
time in the Presbyterian church, occasionally in the old Slate
Hill church, but mostly in the stone house now owned by the
United Bretheren. In 1828, they built a brick church which
served them for forty-four years. In 1844 the two churches of
the united charge reported thirty-two families and a hundred
and thirty-two members, a remarkable number of members in
proportion to the number of families.

In 1845, Mr. McNaughton in conjunction with Mr. Webster
of Philadelphia, withdrew from the Presbytery and Synod,
because of the Synod's lack of orthodoxy in its negotiations
with the Associate Reformed Church in the matter of union.
Both congregations went with him and remained thus for
twelve years. They learned however to their sorrow that no
congregation in our day, can live and prosper in a christian
community, while separated from all ecclesiastical connection
and sympathy. In 1857 Mr. McNaughton left, and they returned
to their old Presbytery, but in a greatly enfeebled condition.
Still on the 11th day of May, 1858, James Bruce was
installed as their pastor, in the hope that they might recuperate.
Mr. McNaughton passed first to the New School Covenanters
and subsequently to the Presbyterian church, as the
result of his ultra orthodoxy.

When the union of 1822 wrecked the Presbytery of Big
Spring, the church in Chambersburg, after the resignation of
Mr. Strong, connected itself with the Presbytery of Mononga-

hela, and was joined with the congregation of Big Spring in a pastoral charge. Alexander Sharp was installed in this charge during the autumn of 1824, and gave to Chambersburg, the one-third of his time till the 11th of September, 1828, when he resigned his pastoral care of this branch and confined himself to Big Spring. On the 8th of April, 1828, Alexander McCahan was received as a probationer from the Seceder Presbytery of Coleraine in Ireland; on the 2d of the following December he was ordained, and on the 26th of the same month was installed as pastor of Chambersburg and Concord, giving two-thirds of his time to the former, and one-third to the latter. This pastoral relation continued only to the 6th of October 1830, when it was dissolved, and Mr. McCahan soon passed to the Presbytery of Monongahela.

The removal of Mr. McCahan in the spring of 1831, practically suspended the functions of the Presbytery, for Mr. Smith, was superannuated, and in February, 1832, died, thus leaving Mr. Sharp as the only minister. To remove the difficulty thus interposed, on the 2d of April, 1834, the Rev. N. C. Weede and his congregations at Blairsville, Bethel, and Brush Valley, in Indiana county, were transferred by the Presbytery of Monongahela to the Presbytery of Big Spring, and on the 5th of the following August, the Presbytery resumed its meetings. Mr. Weede and his pastoral charge continued in this connection till the summer of 1838, when they were returned to their old Presbytery.

On the 3d of August, 1837, Robert Gracey was ordained and installed over the united congregations of Chambersburg and Concord. On the 18th of October, 1843, he was released from the Concord branch, and was installed for that half of his time as pastor of the church at Gettysburg on the 30th of October, 1844. On the 10th October, 1849, Mr. Gracey demitted the Gettysburg church, and gave three-fourths of his time to Chambersburg, and the remaining fourth to Concord as stated supply. On the 20th of October, 1852, he demitted his charge and accepted a call to the Fourth church in Pittsburgh. The Rev. D. T. Carnahan became the stated supply in both Chambersburg and Gettysburg, and so remained for two years, and was succeeded, in the autumn of 1854, by Rev. John R. Warner, who served these churches in the same capacity for three years.

A number of families in and about McConnellsburg, in Fulton county, and connected with the Cove church, became greatly dissatisfied with the position and course of their pastor, Mr. McNaughton, and applied to Presbytery, in the spring of 1852, for supply of preaching. This was granted, and in November of the same year, Mr. Gracey organized them into a congregation of thirteen members, and installed W. Sloan Nelson, Mr. Douglass and Hugh Rankin as their elders. Supply was granted them till after the union and the installation of Mr. Bruce, when they found their relation agreeable and coalesced with their former brethren of the Cove.

It seems both proper and desirable to give a brief sketch of the history of the Covenanters who would not go into the union of 1782, and this is perhaps the most suitable place, as they resided mainly in Franklin county. All the organized Covenanter congregations and their pastors went cordially into the formation of the Associate Reformed Church, but nearly all the little isolated societies did not, and continued their regular weekly society meetings; when they spent two or three hours in singing, and praying, and reading the Scriptures, and in religious conversations, to which was often added the reading of a sermon of some of the old Scotch worthies. Two or three of these were in the upper part of Cumberland county, and four in Franklin county. They isolated themselves from the religious services of all other denominations, worshiped God in their own way, and hoped for better days. Quite a number of families of their own faith came to this country from Scotland and Ireland between 1785 and 1800, although but few of them settled in this Valley. They located principally in the cities of New York, Philadelphia, and Pittsburgh, and in the upper section of South Carolina. Rev. James Reid, about 1788 or '9, came from Scotland as a temporary missionary to survey the ground, and soon returned.

Between 1789 and 1797, Rev. Messrs. McGarragh, King, McKinney, Martin and Gibson arrived. The affairs of the

Church in this country were managed by Messrs. Martin, King and McGarragh as a committee of the Reformed Presbytery of Scotland. In 1798 Messrs. McKinney and Gibson, the only surviving ministers, with several ruling elders, proceeded to the establishment of a judiciary independent of all foreign control, and constituted the "Reformed Presbytery of the United States of North America." Within a few years Messrs. Wylie, Black, McLeod and Donnely joined them, and their prosperity was such that in 1808 they organized a Synod. During all these years the little societies in the Valley grew but little, for the tide of immigration, their only source of increase, flowed in other channels. They had no congregational organization, but existed as a confederacy. Each society would appoint a delegate, and these would meet at stated times, in some central place, generally at the house of Mr. Thompson, on the East Conecocheague, and attend to all the interests of a general nature. In all the meetings of the societies, and of the central committee, when a vote was taken, the youngest member generally voted first, and so on according to juvenility, until the oldest voted last. In process of time, the societies of the Walnut Bottom, of Shippensburg, of Roxbury, and of Mercersburg became extinct as societies, through death and emigration, although individual members remained in all of them.

When an organization took place, most probably between 1805 and 1807, it included the societies of Big Spring, Scotland, Green Castle, Greenwood and Waynesboro'. These had no separate or individual organizations; they were simply inorganic parts of one church, whose central place was Scotland. The latter place was not, and is not yet, a village; it was so called because about 1772, four or five Scotch families settled there upon the creek, and built mills—a grist mill, a saw mill, a sickle mill, and a whisky mill—and as they were all Covenanters, it became a kind of a centre for those of their faith.

In 1816, Robert Lusk, a native of Cumberland county, was ordained and installed as the first pastor of the "Conecocheague congregation." His time was thus divided: "One-fourth of his time in Newville and Walnut Bottom; one-fourth

6

in Shippensburg; one-fourth in Green township, and the remaining fourth in the Lurgan and Waynesburg society; and days for other places to be taken out of the whole, as occasion may serve." Part of Shippensburg's time was subsequently given to Roxbury. John Thompson, John Renfrew, John Steel, and John Scouller were the ruling elders.

Mr. Lusk remained five or six years, and was succeeded in 1824 by Samuel W. Crawford, who preached one-third of his time at Waynesburg; one-third at Fayetteville, and one-third at Scotland. He remained till the spring of 1831. About 1820, a small log church was built at Greenwood, and in 1825, a stone church was erected at Scotland, and as the society had drifted from Greenwood to Fayetteville, a building was put up in 1840 in the latter place. In 1842, Thomas Hannay, an Irish licentiate, was ordained and installed. He remained till the autumn of 1844, when he resigned, and is now a minister of our Church in Canada. During the autumn of 1845, Joshua Kennedy, a native of Franklin county, was ordained and installed as pastor, and remained till May, 1860, when he removed to Delaware county, New York. Since this, the congregation has remained vacant, with an occasional day's preaching in Scotland or Fayetteville, and numbers about thirty members, and some of these are widely scattered. Its future prospects are by no means encouraging.

CUMBERLAND COUNTY.

After Mr. Strong had left Shippensburg, the congregation put itself under the care of the Second Presbytery of Philadelphia, because of its Associate Reformed antecedents, and was supplied by Presbyterian ministers. On the 18th of February, 1824, Rev. Henry R. Wilson, formerly of Silver's Spring was installed as pastor, and so remained till October, 1839. He and the congregation were transferred in April, 1825, to the Presbytery of Carlisle, where it has ever since remained.

In 1838, the Presbytery of Big Spring re-organized a church in Shippensburg, when Henry Carlile and William Means were ordained and installed as ruling elders. In April, 1839, suit was entered for the church building, which was not successful, because of the strange rulings of the judge. Appeal was taken to the Supreme Court, and a new trial was ordered, which proved successful, and on the 14th of November, 1842, the congregation was put in possession of the house, and on the 5th of July, 1843, the Rev. Alex. Sharp, of Big Spring, was installed as pastor for the one-third of his time. The movement was not a success, the English population was monopolized by the well established Presbyterian church of the place, and all else was German. On the 25th of October, 1848, Mr. Sharp resigned and the little society gradually dwindled away, and the church building was leased to the borough, for school purposes, for ninety-nine years, for the sum of one thousand dollars.

After long waiting and many efforts, the Big Spring congregation finally secured a pastor in the person of Alexander Sharp, who was ordained in Pittsburgh by the Presbytery of Monongahela on the 8th of September, 1824, and installed on the 29th of the same month, by Rev. T. Smith, as pastor of Big Spring and Chambersburg; giving two-thirds of his time at a salary of $400 per year to the former, and one-third of his time for $200 to the latter. Mr. Sharp was born and reared in the Big Spring congregation, and after being graduated at Canonsburg, commenced the study of theology under Dr. Mason, and finished under Dr. Riddell. After his resignation of the Shippensburg church he gave all his time to Big Spring, and received the full salary. In 1825, at a congregational meeting it was unanimously resolved, "That in singing the Psalms, the members of the congregation furnish themselves with Psalm books, and that after the reading of the Psalm, and the giving out of the first two lines by the pastor, the congregation continue to sing, uninterrupted by the giving out of the lines." In 1826, the congregation replaced the old stone church with a new brick house, which in that day was regarded as being very superior in beauty, finish, and convenience, and with only a small debt, which was fully discharged in two years.

After several years of declining health, Dr. Sharp died on the 28th of January, 1857, in the sixty-first year of his age, and the thirty-third of his pastorate. He died where he had lived all his days, and among a people which had known his life from his earliest childhood ; and although as a general rule, a prophet is without honor " in his own country, and among his own kin, and his own house," yet the great crowd of mourners around his bier bore ample testimony to the universal belief, that " a prince and a great man had fallen in Israel." He was a man of influence and of power, not only in his own pastoral field, but also in his Synod, which in the seventh year of his ministry elected him as its sole professor of theology, as the successor of Dr. Joseph Kerr ; this appointment he was, however, constrained to decline. In person he was large and robust, of good presence and manly appearance. While his voice was monotonous, and often pitched too high, his style was fluent, and his command of Scripture language was simply amazing. Strangers who heard him but rarely were generally not pleased with him, for his hearers had to be familiar with his peculiarities before they could properly appreciate his wealth of matter. He possessed a strong, clear logical mind, which enabled him to develop his subject clearly, symmetrically, and exhaustively, so that he always gratified his intelligent hearers. And yet his greatest characteristic was a large amount of good common sense, combined with good taste, so that what he said and did was always judicious, appropriate, and to the point. During his last years he became very much interested in prophecy, and gave, perhaps, too much time and space to it, but throughout his whole ministry his preaching was mainly expository and didactic. It was impossible to sit under his ministry, and to remain ignorant of the Bible and its plan of salvation, for he taught a whole Bible, not mere spots and parts ; and he expounded a full system of doctrinal truths, and had no favorite subjects to force his preaching into old well-worn ruts. In labors he was very abundant, for during the first ten years of his ministry he was almost alone in the territory east of the mountains, with seven or eight vacant congregations to be cared for ; all of which he occasionally visited, and as they were widely scattered it involved an amount of horseback riding through heat and cold, sun and rain, which told severely even upon his grand physique, and his subsequent broken health could be clearly traced to some of these exposures.

In the extreme north-western corner of York county stands the small village of Dillsburg, a name which appeared for thirty years in the minutes of the Associate Presbytery of Philadelphia, and yet there was never an Associate organization in that neighborhood. That section of country was settled by Irish as early as 1740, or sooner. They were a mixture of Covenanters, Seceders, and Synod of Ulster families; the last largely predominating. A Presbyterian church was early organized here, by the Presbytery of Donegal, which in 1746 was united with the East Pennsborough (Silver's Spring) church to form a pastoral charge. In the process of time the Reformed and Associate families came in, so that the church included the entire English speaking population. Things continued thus till about 1823 or '5, when, during the ministry of the Rev. N. Todd, "Watt's book of Psalms and Hymns was introduced, in the place of the old version of Psalmody by Rouse." This gave great offence to a number of families, particularly those of Covenanter ancestry, and the O'Hails, the Wilsons, the Blairs, the McCurdys, Mrs. Col. Logan, and a few other families withdrew and joined the Associate church at Carlisle, and invited Mr. Pringle to preach for them occasionally. He gave them the one-fourth of his time as long as he lived. In 1835, James Dunlap, a native of Big Spring, and for some time ruling elder in the Silver's Spring church, for a similar reason, transferred his membership to Carlisle, and attended services at Dillsburg. There was no church organization, nor church building, no bench of elders, nor administration of the Lord's Supper. It was simply a preaching station, and, like Dickinson, its communicants were members of the Carlisle church, and the subsequent history of the three places is the same. In 1826, Carlisle reported fifty-two families and eighty communicants, and it is doubtful whether at any subsequent time they exceeded this number.

Francis Pringle was born in Fifeshire, Scotland, in 1747, studied theology under Moncrieff, of Alloa, was licensed by the Presbytery of Kirkcaldy before he was twenty-one years old, and was soon sent to supply the Associate congregation of

Gilnakirk, near Belfast, in Scotland. Here he was ordained
and installed in August, 1772, and remained as pastor till 1798,
when part of his congregation sympathized with the "Irish
Rebellion," and as he was strongly loyal, trouble ensued, and he
resigned, and during the next year sailed for New York,
where he landed on the 26th of September, 1799. He was installed in Carlisle on the 27th of August, 1802; served the Associate Synod for twenty-five years as its first Stated Clerk,
until he was almost eighty years old. He resigned his charge,
and preached his farewell sermon on the 14th of May, 1832, and
then went to New York city to make his home with his only
surviving son. In consequence of a fall, he died on the 2d of
November, 1833, in the 85th year of his age, and the 64th year
of his ministry. He was an instructive preacher, a strong
Church man, and a diligent laborer, and was universally
respected. The Hon. W. B. McClure, of Pittsburgh, who
was brought up under his ministry, says of him: "His character was an institution in the sphere in which he moved.
He scattered cheerfulness, and love, and light wherever he
went. We looked at him as a star whose light was borrowed
from a source beyond the sun."

In May, 1833, sundry residents in Wheatfield township, near
the mouth of Sherman's creek, in Perry county, petitioned the
Associate Presbytery of Philadelphia for supply of preaching.
The ultimate result of this was a church organization, which
was completed on the 24th of June, 1834, when Mr. Adams
ordained and installed Alexander Gaily, Robert G. Stephens,
Alexander Garret and John Duncan as ruling elders. This
congregation took the name of Unity, but when they erected
a new house, and located in the neighboring village of Petersburg, they assumed the name of that place, and when the
corporate name of Petersburg was changed to Duncannon,
they also changed their name to Duncannon. Two years previous to this organization, some families in Juniata township,
near Milford, applied for a supply of preaching, and in due
time they received a kind of half organization. This station
was sometimes joined to the Unity congregation as a northern

wing, and sometimes it acted independently, but it never made much progress in either capacity.

In 1834, the Presbytery formed Unity and Carlisle into a pastoral charge, and this relation continued for twenty-three years. On the 7th of May, 1835, three different calls were laid upon the table of Presbytery for the pastoral services of Alexander T. McGill. One was from Carlisle and Unity, another from Stone Valley and connections, and the third from Baltimore. Mr. McGill declined to decide between these calls, and left the whole matter with Presbytery, which decided in favor of Carlisle and Unity. Mr. McGill was accordingly ordained and installed as pastor of this charge on the 30th of September, 1835, in the Dickinson stone church. His services were satisfactory, and, under the circumstances, successful, but on the 14th of September, 1837, he offered his resignation of the charge because of the labor and exposure involved, particularly in the winter season, in supplying four different and distant preaching places. This tender was not acted upon till the 2d of November, when it was accepted, and at the same meeting, a call was presented to him from the newly formed Second congregation of Philadelphia. This call he took under consideration, and agreed to supply its pulpit during the succeeding winter.

On the 2d of May, 1838, a second call was given Mr. McGill from Carlisle and Unity, which he accepted upon the condition that no present arrangements should be made for his installation. He assumed at once the charge of these congregations, and everything went on smoothly till the meeting of Presbytery at Mercersburg, on the 24th of October of the same year, when he returned the call and asked for a certificate of dismission from the Associate Church, upon the ground that for two years doubts had been growing in his mind as to the truth of that Church's peculiar teachings upon the subjects of Occasional Hearing, Communion and Psalmody. The final result of the Presbytery's action was his suspension from the ministry and the communion of the Church. He asked for a certified copy of the minutes in his case, which was granted. This he took to the Presbytery of Carlisle and asked for admission, well aware of the fact that that document would secure him a more

hearty reception than an ordinary certificate of transfer. He
was received, and immediately accepted a call to the Second
Presbyterian church of Carlisle. Two of his elders, Messrs.
Clark and Davidson, and several families went with him, which
caused a serious and permanent injury to the Associate congregation which he left. As Mr. McGill had not been accused of
any immorality, nor of any serious overt act of unfaithfulness
to the testimony of his Church, it will now be very generally
conceded that the Associate Presbytery of Philadelphia did,
in this case, act hastily and with undue severity. And yet it
is but justice to the Presbytery to say that its action must not
be judged from what simply appears upon its minutes; for its
members had heard things, extra-judicially, which influenced
their minds, and led them into the belief that Mr. McGill had
not acted with sufficient candor and straight-forwardness. At
his communion in Unity, a few days before, he denied any in-
tention of such a movement, and made an appointment for his
future preaching as usual, while at the same time it was asserted in Carlisle that he had entertained with favor, proposals
made by certain parties in the Second Presbyterian church of
that place. The writer happened to be one of Mr. McGill's
parishioners at this very time, and entertained for him then
and ever since, nothing but feelings of kindness and of good
will, yet he always did believe that Mr. McGill's doubts, upon
the subject of Psalmody at least, could not be two years old,
for within much less time than that, while "explaining" the
eighteenth Psalm, he called the congregation's attention to the
fact that this Psalm was a repetition of the twenty-second
chapter of Second Samuel, and asserted that no sufficient reason could be given why this Psalm should be recorded twice in
the Bible, except that the Holy Spirit designed to use it in the
praises of the Church, and to make this proper or lawful, it
was necessary to transfer it to the authorized Book of Praise;
and concluded with the remark that he had no doubt but that
the saints in glory would praise God in the language of David
and Asaph. This was more than loyalty to the standards of
the Associate Church, for they nowhere confine the matter of
praise to one hundred and fifty Psalms, to the exclusion of

other Scriptures. It cannot be regarded as either improper or unkind to allude to these things in this place, for Dr. McGill, after nursing his grievances for thirty-five years, saw fit to resurrect this whole matter, in a very offensive way and with no little bad taste, in his letter to the Re-union of *all* the Presbyterians of Cumberland Valley, which took place in the summer of 1874, at Oakville.

On the 26th of March, 1841, the Rev. D. Anderson accepted a call to Carlisle and Unity, and was installed in the Carlisle church on the 28th of October; but his pastorate was very short. In the following May he went to Synod in Philadelphia, accompanied by his daughter, who was going to Baltimore. He engaged her passage on a boat which plied between the two places, and having put her aboard, while going down the gangway, which was wet with rain, he slipped, and to recover himself, he set down his closed umbrella with such force as to break the handle, and then falling upon the upright piece received a severe wound in his side, from which he died in a few hours. Mr. Anderson was a native of Scotland, and was held in high esteem by his friends as a scholar, as a man, and as a minister.

In January, 1844, Mr. T. R. Simpson became stated supply in Carlisle and Unity, and on the 10th of the following October was ordained and installed as pastor; the services taking place in the latter place. Mr. Simpson's pastorate was as successful as could be expected under the circumstances; but excessive emigration continued to deplete the congregations till 1855, when he resigned, and removed to New Jefferson, Ohio, and is now resident in Allegheny City.

After this Carlisle received very little supply, and virtually disbanded in 1858. The younger members gradually united with the nearest Presbyterian church, and the older died off one after another, until very few if any remain. The Dillsburg branch had no property to dispose off, and the church property in Carlisle was sold by the Presbytery in 1863, for $1,325, to the Winebrennerians. The ground upon which the Dickinson church was built, was donated for a specific purpose by Mr. Moore, and when that purpose is abandoned it will of course revert to his heirs.

ADAMS COUNTY.

Mr. McLean and the churches of Gettysburg and the Hill, retained their connection with the Presbytery of Philadelphia when it united with the Presbyterian church in 1822, and continued to do so until that Presbytery dissolved in 1824, and when the Presbytery of Baltimore refused to receive Mr. Duncan in 1825, Mr. McLean, his very special and intimate friend, declined to offer his certificate to the Presbytery of Carlisle, and joined with Duncan, Chambers, and Jewett, in forming the "Independent Presbytery." When he returned to his charge from the meeting of the Synod of Baltimore, where Duncan's appeal was not sustained, he held up his Bible before his congregation and said: "That is all that I have left, and if you are satisfied to retain me with that, I will remain with you; if not, I will be obliged to seek a home elsewhere." His people were very much attached to him, and sympathized warmly with him, and acceded to his terms. There was no formal transfer of the congregation, and it retained its old name of Associate Reformed. Things remained thus until the 25th of January, 1840, when a congregational meeting was held, but without any public intimation of its object. Eighteen members attended this meeting at which it was resolved to apply to the Legislature for a change of name. In this they were successful, and their legal name was changed to "the Independent Church of Gettysburg." But the change of civil name did not bring ecclesiastical prosperity, and in 1842 Dr. McLean terminated his connection with them, and went first to a Presbyterian church in Baltimore, then to a Reformed Dutch congregation at Fort Plain, in New York, and then took charge of a Female Seminary in Indianapolis, Indiana, where he died on the 4th of July, 1860, in the 74th year of his age. He was a man of very decided abilities, and was greatly esteemed.

Gettysburg and the Hill now found themselves without a pastor, and without any Churchly relations, and soon began to realize their loneliness and destitution. They must look somewhere, and as they had retained the forms and customs of their former days, they naturally turned to the Associate Reformed Presbytery of Big Spring. So, on the 18th of August, 1842, they sent commissioners to that Presbytery, soliciting a supply of preaching, and asking upon what terms they could be received under its care. A supply was granted, and for information as terms of union, they were referred to the Confession of Faith. On the 18th of April, 1843, they were formally and heartily received, and have so remained ever since. On the 15th of November, 1843, they gave a call to Joseph H. Pressly, which was declined. On the 18th of September, 1844, Presbytery joined these congregations with Chambersburg in a pastoral charge, and on the 30th of October, Mr. Gracey was installed as pastor for half of his time. This relation continued till the 10th of October, 1849. For three years they were again dependent upon the Presbytery for supplies, during which time a call given to James Greer was declined. In the autumn of 1852, they were again united to Chambersburg, and the Rev. D. T. Carnahan served both places for two years as stated supply. He was followed for three years by the Rev. John R. Warner as stated supply. Mr. Warner was opposed to the contemplated union of the Associate Reformed and Associate Churches, and in 1857, accepted a call to a Presbyterian Church in the immediate vicinity, and did everything in his power to have our churches disorganize, so that their families might unite with his church and the Presbyterian congregation in Gettysburg. In this he was not successful, although he effected some mischief, and the congregations went cordially into the union which formed the United Presbyterian Church.

YORK COUNTY.

As already stated elsewhere, a number of the families of the Associate Reformed church in Lower Chanceford, became very much dissatisfied with the action of their Presbytery (the Philadelphia), in reference to the union of 1822, and sought connection with the Associate congregation of Guinston. For their accommodation a church was organized in Lower Chanceford, on the 13th of August, 1823, and Mr. Gordon gave to them the one-fourth of his time. Most of these families returned to the Associate Reformed congregation in a few years, after its prospects became more encouraging, still the organization was kept up and in connection with Guinston, till after the union of 1858. On the 20th of October, 1825, Mr. Gordon's relation to these churches was dissolved, and he removed to Putnam, New York, and subsequently to Johnstown of the same state, where he died suddenly on the 20th of August, 1845. Mr. Gordon was a man of melancholy temperament, but of more than ordinary ability as a preacher and as a writer.

During the latter part of 1825, Guinston gave a call to Mr. Thomas Goodwillie, which was declined; and the 13th of April 1830, they did the same to Horatio Thompson with the same result. After two other abortive efforts, they finally succeeded, on the 11th of September, 1833, in having John Adams installed as their pastor. For more than twenty years he discharged the duties of his ministry with peace, and comfort, and reasonable success. On the 26th of April, 1855, he demitted his charge because of declining health and of the frailties of old age, although he lived to the 14th of January, 1862, when he quietly passed away without an hour's premonition. He was a good man and an instructive preacher, although not specially attractive in his manner.

On the 14th of August, 1856, Francis McBurney was ordained and installed as Mr. Adam's successor, and he and his charge went heartily into the union of 1858, and thus laid aside the ecclesiastical name which Guinston or Muddy Creek had borne for more than a hundred years.

The union of 1822, was almost a death blow to the Associate Reformed churches in Lower Chanceford and Hopewell. Some were discouraged and went into the Presbyterian church, others united with the Associate church at Guinston, but a faithful few remained in each place, who resolved to wait and see what time and Providence would do for them. They turned their backs upon the departing Presbytery of Philadelphia, with which they had always been connected, and when the Presbytery of Big Spring was re-organized, they united themselves with it, and have so remained till the present time. For several years their supply of preaching was very limited, but it gradually became more abundant, and they strengthened in numbers and resources, so that they felt able to support a pastor, and on the

30th of August, 1843, D. B. Jones was ordained and installed as their spiritual guide. This relation continued till the 30th of April, 1847, when Mr. Jones resigned, and during the following year left the Presbytery. On the 25th of October, 1848, William Carlile was ordained and installed in this same field, and although surrounded with some discouragements he did a good work, but was compelled to resign on the 15th of May, 1856, because of ill health. On the 6th of May, 1857, Joseph Boyd was ordained and installed as the next pastor, but his incumbency lasted only until the 14th of the following April. The union with the Associate Church which was consummated in May, made a re-casting of the pastorates in York county both possible and desirable.

JUNIATA AND MIFFLIN COUNTIES.

When the crash of 1822 left Mr. Smith alone in the Presbytery of Big Spring, he and his congregations in Fermanagh and Tuscarora sought the care of the Presbytery of Monongahela, until the installation of Mr. Sharp resuscitated his old Presbytery. But now he had become an old man, and his day of labor was fast drawing to its close. He had labored well and successfully, and had maintained his congregations in good condition, notwithstanding the many difficulties with which he had to contend. When he first took charge of Fermanagh in 1806, it had thirty-six families and ninety-four members; in 1830, it had thirty-nine families and ninety members. Tuscarora he organized about 1801, and left it with fifty families and a hundred and five members. During the last two years of Mr. Smith's life, he was so frail as not to be able to perform much work, and as there was but one other minister in the Presbytery, he could receive but little help. On the 12th of February, 1832, he died in the seventy-seventh year of his age, and the fifty-sixth of his ministry.

Mr. Smith was born in Ireland, and like all the Seceder ministers of his day, was educated in Scotland. He became pastor of the congregation of Ahanghel, in the county of Antrim, which he served for a number of years, and then emigrated to the United States in the early part of 1799. He landed at New Castle, Delaware, and for a year made that the home of his family.

In the spring of 1800, he moved up to York county, Pennsylvania, and supplied Chanceford and Hopewell for a year, and in 1801, he was installed for half his time as pastor of Tuscarora, where he bought a farm, upon which he ever afterwards lived, and where he died. He was small in stature, of ruddy complexion, had a warm temperament, and was very temperate in all his habits. He was cultured and gentlemanly in his manners, and in every position and relation in life which he was called to occupy he exhibited the graces of the active but humble christian. He was a strong Churchman, and was rooted and grounded in his attachments to the distinctive doctrines of the Associate Reformed Church, and opposed at all times, every attempt at union with the Presbyterian Church. When that union did partially take place, to the injury of Presbytery, he stuck by his old banner, and was the means of preventing worse consequences. As a preacher, he was good and instructive, and no mean master of tender pathos and fiery denunciation.

On the 18th of June, 1835, James Shields was ordained and installed over the congregations of Fermanagh and Tuscarora, dividing his time equally between the two places, and making his residence within the bounds of the former. Shortly after Mr. Shields' settlement, a restless spirit of emigration showed itself in his section of country, and his congregations suffered severely from the removal of whole families, so that in spite of respectable accessions, they steadily decreased in their number of members.

After the resignation of Mr. Brown, the congregation of Concord remained vacant until the 28th of December, 1828, when Alexander McCahan was installed for the two-fifths of his time in connection with Chambersburg. This pastorate lasted till the 6th of October, 1830, when Mr. McCahan resigned and soon afterwards took charge of the congregation at Canonsburg. On the 3d of August, 1837, Robert Gracey was installed as pastor in connection with Chambersburg. In consequence of the long ride and bad roads which separate between these places, he resigned his care of Concord on the 18th of October, 1843, although before his removal to Pittsburg he supplied it again for a season. Their dependence upon Presbytery for word and ordinance continued till 1856, when the Rev. D. B. Jones returned to the Presbytery and ministered to them as stated supply.

Shortly after his settlement in Fermanagh, Mr. Logan began to preach occasionally to a few families in the valley of the Kishacoquillas, within what is now Mifflin county. The result was the organization of a small church about 1790, composed of the McDowells, the Camerons, the Flemings, the Cumminses, the Bickets, the Brahams, the Samples, the Bairds, and the McKees, the most of whom had come from Scotland. Hugh Braham, Alexander Cameron, and James Fleming were ordained as elders. They came to form a part of Mr. Logan's charge, and were supplied by him as long as he was able to ride that far. During the years of 1805 and 1806, they were supplied part of the time by William Adair, before his ordination and removal to Virginia. After this they were dependent upon the occasional services of Mr. Smith, and during the year 1809, formed the one-fifth part of his pastoral charge. For ten or fifteen years longer he preached for them three or four days per year, which was not sufficient to keep them up against the inroads of death and emigration, so that the enterprise gradually died out.

And yet the cause did not entirely perish, for some of the families still remained and continued faithful to their religious convictions. About the year 1825, a difficulty occurred in the neighboring Presbyterian church, over the introduction of hymns into their public services, which threw off sundry families which joined with these remaining ones, and they applied to the Associate Presbytery of Philadelphia for a supply of preaching, which was granted, and John G. Smart visited them in 1828. During the winter of 1832–3, they were regularly organized as a congregation by the Rev. William McElwee, when Col. William Cummins and Major William Ramsey were ordained as ruling elders.

At this same time a similar movement was made by James

McConnell and others, in and near Lewistown, situated at the mouth of Kishacoquillas Creek. In the winter of 1832–3 they were also organized into a congregation by the Rev. W. McElwee, and John L. Porter and Samuel W. Stewart were ordained as their ruling elders. On the 8th of April. 1834, these two congregations were united by Presbytery with Stone Valley, so as to form one pastoral charge, and for many years these three congregations have substantially a common history.

HUNTINGDON COUNTY.

The congregation of Huntingdon, including its important out station at Manor Hill, continued reasonably prosperous up to the 23d of August, 1825, when its pastor, Mr. Smith, died. It numbered at that time about one hundred members, but it had now seen its best days, and was never favored with another pastor.

The Rev. Thomas Smith was a native of Dumfries, in Scotland, was educated at Edinburg, and in 1790, was ordained and appointed by the Associate Synod as a missionary to the United States. This appointment he finally declined, but subsequently, about the year 1800, he came to this country upon his own responsibility. He traveled among the churches till the autumn of 1811, without receiving any call, and then settled down in Huntingdon, where he spent the remainder of his life. He possessed a fair mind, and was strongly attached to the doctrines of his Church, but his greatest strength lay in a kind and hospitable disposition, which made him a very industrious and sympathetic pastor.

The inflow of Associate families was mainly into the upper part of Stone Valley, so that about 1830, a new preaching station was there opened, and for the accommodation of this branch, the Stone Valley church, one-half mile east of McAlevy's Fort, was built in 1832. Here the communion was administered for the first time in November, 1833, by Dr. Beveridge; and from this onward this branch acted as an independent congregation, although it was never distinctively organized. As Huntingdon decreased and its branch at Manor Hill increased, the latter inherited the organization of the former; and as Manor Hill decreased and its branch near McAlevy's Fort increased, so this latter inherited this transmitted organization, and Stone Valley thus received its congregational autonomy upon the principle of the survival of the fittest. Robert Cummins and James Semple were about this time ordained as ruling elders, and in 1833, the congregation first appeared upon the roll of Synod, and was credited with forty-six members.

As already stated, Presbytery, in 1834, united Stone Valley, Kishacoquillas and Lewistown into a pastoral charge. This left the congregation in the town of Huntingdon with only thirty-six members, and in an isolated and helpless condition. In 1838, they gave a call to Rev. David Thompson to become their pastor, but this he declined, and the congregation never made another effort to secure a pastor. Death and emigration without any immigration of those of their faith, gradually diminished their numbers, until in utter discouragement, they sold their house in 1847, and in a few years became extinct. Thus perished through the shifting of population, and some unwise management the oldest and at one time the largest congregation in the respectable and growing town of Huntingdon.

In May, 1835, the united charge of Stone Valley, Kishacoquillas, and Lewistown gave a call to Alexander T. McGill, which was not successful. In October of the same year another call was given to William Galbraith, which was also declined. In February, 1836, a call was given to John S. Easton, who accepted it, and was ordained and installed, on the 5th of May, at the Stone Valley church. He preached one-fourth of his time in Lewistown, one-fourth at Kishacoquillas, and one-half at Stone Valley. Preaching one Sabbath per month may keep a country congregation alive, where there is no competition or antagonism, but in a place of the size and activity of Lewistown, it is simply slow starvation; and so it proved in this case. Lewistown did not receive accessions sufficient to compensate for its natural losses, and gradually declined until the 17th of May, 1842, when Presbytery united it and Kishacoquillas into one church under the name of Reedsville. On the 20th of February, 1855, Mr. Easton resigned his official relation

7

to these churches, to take charge of the congregations at Scroggsfield and Yellow Creek, Ohio, to which he had been called the previous autumn. Stone Valley had at this time ninety-six members. The congregation of Kishacoquillas built, in 1841, a neat brick church in the village of Reedsville; and previous to this the congregation of Lewistown had bought a church from the United Brethren. After the consolidation of these two congregations into one, the church in Lewistown became ultimately useless, and the united congregation made an attempt to sell it, which was resisted by one of its old elders; and it was only after a long litigation and an enabling act of the Legislature, that it was sold for seven hundred dollars. So Lewistown, like Huntingdon, is now without trace or memorial of the Associate Church.

After the departure of Mr. Easton, a call was given to Mr. J. W. McFarland, which was declined. These congregations came heartily into the union of 1858, and in the reconstruction of Presbyteries they came under the supervision of the Big Spring Presbytery of the United Presbyterian Church.

SCHUYLKILL AND CARBON COUNTIES.

Early in the year 1849, a petition was received by the Associate Reformed Presbytery of Big Spring, from a number of families in Pottsville, Schuylkill county, earnestly asking for preaching. They were all immigrants from Ireland, who could not in that place find the precise type of Presbyterianism to which they had been accustomed. Their petition was liberally answered, and on the 17th of January, 1851, a church was organized of twenty-nine members, and Samuel Thompson and James G. Cochran were ordained to the eldership. An appeal for help had already been made to the churches of the Presbytery, and with such aid as they had thus received, but mainly from their own resources, they entered, on the 20th of April of the same year, a very commodious house of worship, with a seating capacity of four hundred. The Rev. D. T. Carnahan commenced supplying them in 1850 and was, on the 22d of October, 1851, installed as pastor. He resigned on the 28th of September, 1852, and John R. Warner was ordained and installed as his successor on the 13th of April, 1853, but his pastorate continued only to the 30th of September of the same year. William II. Prestley commenced supplying them early in 1855, and that his usefulness might be increased, he was ordained on the 12th of June, *sine titulo*. He remained as their stated supply till October of the following year, since which they were dependent upon occasional supply.

In February, 1851, application was made to the Presbytery of Big Spring, by some Irish families residing at Summit Hill, Carbon county, for a supply of word and ordinance, similar to what they had enjoyed in their native land. This request was generously met, and a full supply was sent them for the summer and winter, and during the winter some time, a church was regularly organized. During the summer of 1852, they gave a call to the Rev. James Johnson, D. D., who, having finished his long and successful pastorate in Mansfield, Ohio, had returned to his native home in York county, to spend the evening of his days. Dr. Johnson supplied them for a season, but declined the labors and responsibilities of pastoral care. They never provided for themselves a church building, neither did they make any further effort to procure a pastor. Both these churches were mainly dependent upon a floating population, which had been attracted by the extensive coal mines in their vicinity, and which was subject to constant fluctuation. After a few years of good promise things took a change, and both enterprises failed. Still it was the belief of some who were in a favorable position to know, that Pottsville migh have succeeded if it had been more wisely managed, for it had a basis of permanent families, and the size and growing importance of the place, promised a gradual increase of the same kind. The experience of the Associate Reformed Church has uniformly shown that in all new enterprises, wisdom is of more importance and in the end more successful than brilliant talents.

MISCELLANEOUS.

On the 13th of August, 1828, a Rev. James Wilson was received as a member of Presbytery, but during the next year, he left for Washington Presbytery, New York, where he did not stay long enough to become a member of its Synod.

April 28, 1829, a petition was received from James P. Ramsey, Mrs. M. McLandburg and others in Philadelphia, asking to be recognized as a vacancy, and to be supplied with preaching. This petition was granted, and for a year they received considerable supply, but the removal of Mr. McCahan and the failure of Mr. Smith from age, left Mr. Sharp alone in Presbytery, so in 1830, he transferred Philadelphia to the Presbytery of New York.

The General Synod of 1851 sent down to Presbyteries certain overtures in reference to Church Government. Presbytery, at a full meeting of its members on the 14th of April, 1852, gave the following answer, viz:

"1st. That no alteration be made in the ratio of Presbyterial representation to General Synod.

"2d. That General Synod be recommended to strike out in Book 1st, on Church Government, Chapter 3d, Section 1st, and paragraph 2d, the word 'male,' and insert the word 'communing,' in its place.

"3d. That in temporalities, the right of voting be extended to pew-holders, or supporters of the ordinances, who have no voice in any other congregation: Provided, This right be not so extended as to affect the election or dismission of Pastors or the election of Elders or Deacons."

These same subjects were re-overtured by the Synod, and Presbytery, at a meeting held at Pottsville, April 13, 1853, when there were only two ministers and two elders present, took the following action, viz:

"1st. That our Standards be so altered that the word 'male' be stricken out in reference to church members voting for church officers—ayes, 2; nays, 2.

"2d. That our standards be so altered as to allow pew-holders, and persons contributing to the support of the gospel, to vote in the temporalities of the church: Provided, Such vote do not affect the settlement or removal of the pastor—ayes, 1; nays, 3.

"3d. That the ratio of Presbyterial representation in General Synod remain unaltered—yeas, 4; nays, 0."

The old system of holding diets of catechism, and of making regular annual family visits, for the purpose of individual instruction and prayer, was still kept up in all the churches of the Presbytery, although it became very manifest that it must eventually yield to the more modern system of prayer meetings and Sabbath schools. Facts have shown that these two systems do antagonize each other, and yet it is exceedingly difficult to see why such should be the case. Both systems have their advantages and their disadvantages, and there is certainly no sufficient reason why the Church should not avail itself of the advantages of both.

All these churches in their early days, before they had settled pastors, were more or less in the habit of meeting on their vacant Sabbaths for prayer and praise, at which time a sermon of some Scotch worthy was frequently read. These meetings necessarily ceased when a pastor was installed, and in but very few instances were there any other meetings instituted for prayer on a week day, and in no case more frequently than once in the month.

All this has now changed, and week day prayer meetings and lecture meetings have become the rule, and very much to the spiritual profit of the people. And so with Sabbath schools. A few years ago they were almost unknown, but now are in all the churches, and since their lessons have become systematic and uniform, are imparting a large amount of biblical instruction to the youth of our churches, and are proving equally profitable to the adult members by exacting of them a more careful and diligent study of the Scriptures, in helping their children to prepare their lessons, or in qualifying themselves to teach in the school.

CHAPTER V.

UNION OF 1858.

THE members of the Presbytery of Big Spring interested themselves in the "Union of the Reformed Churches," from the very incipiency of the movement in 1838, when the first convention of delegates from the General Synod of the Reformed Presbyterian Church, and from the Associate Reformed Synods of the West and of New York, was held in Pittsburgh. And when the Associate Church joined in, and annual conferences were held, Dr. Sharp, our senior presbyter, was frequently selected by his Synod as one of its delegates. The position of the Presbytery was always in favor of this union, and upon the most acceptable terms which could be secured; believing that there was not good and sufficient reason why these Scottish churches, of one origin, of one faith, of one worship, and of one practice, should remain separated. While the Presbytery was willing to concede much to others, and to accept in the basis of union things that it might deem unnecessary or superfluous, yet it always had a very decided opinion of its own, as to the form and matter of the standards of the United Church. It was in favor of the shortest and simplest basis that would be compatible with fidelity to the truth as received by the Divine Spririt.

The following extracts from the action of the Presbytery, taken, April 13, 1853, upon the basis of union then before the churches, will give a fair illustration of its views from first to last:

"Inasmuch as faith in human testimony or uninspired history ought not to be required as a term of church fellowship, and as our profession and practice ought to be drawn immediately from the inspired volume, and not from the doctrines of Reformers, decrees of Councils, and traditions of men; we are of opinion that the first party of the Basis should be omitted. What they believed, taught, and practiced, as far as was clearly required by God's word, can be as easily deduced from the Sacred Scriptures, as from their histories, and with less danger of mistake, and with authority not to be called in question.

"The history of times, of men, and of things, since the close of revelation, can be made to answer a valuable end, without making *it* and *faith in it*, a ground of church fellowship.

"It occurs to us, that, as the perversion or denial of doctrines in the Confession of Faith is deemed to be the only reason for adding the testimony, those things in it that are as easily denied and quickly perverted as the corresponding part of the Confession, cannot answer any valuable purpose. If the Standards we have be thought defective, ambiguous, or heretical, an amended Confession is called for, rather than a new Testimony; and while we agree to take for the present, much that we think redundant, we wish to be understood not as thinking that'any part of our Standard is beyond review and amendments by the Church. Another general remark is that we prefer a didactic or declaratory style, to one polemic or argumentative, not only because the object is as fully obtained by the former as the latter method, but on account of the liability to introduce reasonings not sanctioned in the word, and perplexing to the conscience.

When the Associate and the Associate Reformed Churches united on the 26th of May, 1858, in Pittsburgh, and formed the United Presbyterian Church of North America, all the ministers and all the congregations then in connection with these Churches, between the Allegheny mountain and the Susquehanna river, went into this union promptly and heartily, and their ecclesiastical names, which had been living realities for many years, were now given over to the domain of history, for the stream which had been divided by an island for three-quarters of a century, had come together to flow in a deeper and a broader channel under a new name.

CHAPTER VI.

1858—1879.

THE Presbytery of Big Spring, under the care of the Synod of Pittsburgh, and General Assembly of the United Presbyterian Church of North America, was constituted, on June the 8th, 1859, at Newville, Cumberland county. It was composed of the following ministers and congregations, viz: John Adams, James Shields, Joseph McKee, Dargo B. Jones, Francis McBurney, William Carlile, Joseph Boyd, James Bruce, William McElwee, and John M. Adair—ministers; Mercersburg, The Cove, Chambersburg, Big Spring, Gettysburg, The Hill, Guinston, Chanceford, Hopewell, Petersburg, Mexico, Reedsville, Stone Valley, Tuscarora, Concord, and Pottsville. In all, ten ministers and sixteen congregations.

The union found the congregation in the Cove in a very unhappy condition. Mr. McNaughton's ten or twelve years of separation from the Associate Presbytery of Philadelphia, and his opposition to any union with the Associate Reformed Church, gave growing offence to many of his parishioners, and, particularly to those in the Cove. Years before the union, a portion of these, as we have already seen, applied to the Associate Reformed Presbytery of Big Spring, for an organization and a supply of preaching, and were successful in both. At a subsequent period, another part of them applied to their old Presbytery of Philadelphia for re-admission, and were also successful. This left a moiety or less of the original congregation adhering to Mr. McNaughton in his ecclesiastical isolation. At this stage and just preceding the union, Mr. McNaughton resigned, and eventually found his way into the Presbyterian Church, and left his little congregation ecclesiastically nowhere. When the union was consummated a few ministers and congregations of the Associate Church refused to enter it, and perpetuated a small residuary Associate Synod, and the independent portion of the Cove congregation sought and obtained admission to this Synod, and has so continued ever since, and is now know as the Associate congregation of the Cove. They have received occasional supplies until in the summer of 1877, when the Rev. Mr. Houston was installed as pastor for two-thirds of his time. The congregation consists of eleven families, and about twenty-four communicants of intelligent and excellent people.

All the other portions of the original congregations of the Cove and Mercersburg went into the union, and united in giving a call to James Bruce, who, on the 11th of May, 1858, was ordained and installed as their pastor. The settlement was the means of great good every way to these congregations, for it harmonized and united them, and gave them life and hope by bringing them into warm and active Church relations. In April, 1863, Mr. Bruce resigned and took charge of the church at Andes, N. Y., where he still resides. On the 7th of October, 1865, a call was moderated for Robert G. Ferguson, which he accepted, and on the 1st of July, 1866, he took charge of the congregations, although he was not ordained and installed till the 17th of the following October. During the summer of 1872, the congregation at Mecersburg erected a new church building of more than ordinary comfort and neatness. On the 29th of June, 1874, Mr. Ferguson resigned to take charge of the church at Butler, which he still serves. On the 11th of November, 1878, J. E. Black was ordained and installed as pastor of these congregations, and while they are not numerically strong, and their surroundings do not promise great increase, still they are intelligently attached to the Church, and earnest in their endeavors to promote its prosperity.

In the early autumn of 1858, the united congregations of Gettysburg and Chambersburg gave a call to William McElwee, which was accepted, and he was ordained and installed on the 10th of November, as their pastor. The Gettysburg congregation developed considerable enterprise, and remodeled their church building and purchased a parsonage. In the spring of 1860, Mr. McElwee offered the resignation of his charge, for the avowed purpose that each congregation might supply itself with a pastor.

But as the congregations were not anxious for this, the Presbytery declined to accept. Mr. McElwee, however, did not give up his project, and finally succeed in having the Presbytery, on the 11th of September, 1861, release him from Chambersburg, and give all his time to Gettysburg. There is no evidence that Chambersburg was consulted in this movement, and there might be a difference of opinion whether the Presbytery under such circumstances had the right to make the change. The policy of the course was certainly questionable, and its wisdom was never made manifest by its fruits. About this time, and mainly through the efforts of Mr. McElwee, the Hill church abandoned its distinctive organization, and the old Marsh Creek congregation, after an existence of a hundred years, becomes an integral part of the congregation of Gettysburg. In the early spring of 1863, Mr. Elwee, without the knowledge of his Presbytery or consent of his people, set out on a prospecting tour in the Presbyterian Church. When he had closed a bargain with a small congregation in the suburbs of Philadelphia, he sent to Presbytery the resignation of his charge of Gettysburg and asked for a certificate of transfer to the Presbyterian Church. On the 10th of April the first was readily accepted, and the latter was also granted in connection with a resolution of censure for the irregularity of his course.

During the first three days of the succeeding July, the terrible battle of Gettysburg took place, when a hundred and fifty thousand soldiers, tens of thousands of horses, and immense trains of baggage wagons and artillery, were concentrated and manœuvred in and around the town. The wheat was just ready for the reaper, the corn was half grown, and every thing in which the husbandman had an interest was flourishing. The result of the fierce struggle was to the farmers very disastrous. Their growing crops were utterly ruined, their fences were broken down, their live stock was swept away, and in some instances their barns and even their houses were burned, and the churches were turned into hospitals. If the battle did bring joy and hope to the nation, it also brought sorrow and weeping to very many of the inhabitants of the neighborhood, for ruin and desolation now rested upon the fertile fields where ripening grain and pasturing flocks but yesterday gave promise of a full and abundant future.

A large part of the United Presbyterian congregation consisted of farmers, and in their loss and distress was the church severely tried. It was cast down, but not destroyed, for after a season of recuperation, they gave a call to James S. Woodburn, who accepted, and was ordained and installed on the 10th of May, 1864, as pastor in Gettysburg. This pastorate was very short, for on the 7th of the following March, it was dissolved, and Mr. Woodburn followed his predecessors into the Presbyterian Church. Realizing that the congregation was not able to sustain a pastor all this time, the Presbytery united with it the congregation of Duncannon, in Perry county, when a call was given to W. A. Findley, and declined.

On the second Tuesday of April, 1868, the Rev. John Jamison was installed as pastor of the united charge. Subsequently, the congregation of Hopewell, in York county, was substituted for Duncannon, and as thus arranged, Mr. Jamison still holds the charge.

The resignation of Mr. McElwee in the autumn of 1861, left the congregation of Chambersburg in an unfortunate position, for there was no other congregation with which it could be associated, and it was utterly unable to support a pastor alone; and the continuous Germanizing of the community, and the disquietude necessarily arising from its location on "the border" in the Great Rebellion, made its prospects still more gloomy. It lay within an easy distance of both Antietam and Gettysburg, and its farmers were repeatedly losers by the raids and invasions of the enemy until the 30th of July, 1864, when the greater and better part of Chambersburg was burnt by General McCausland, and among the hundreds of houses then given to the torch was the United Presbyterian church.

This loss, in connection with the partial or entire impoverishment of nearly all its members, proved fatal to this old organization. To begin and build anew, with hopes of permanence, appeared to be clearly impossible under existing circumstances, and no effort to recuperate has since been made.

The congregation has never been formally disbanded by Presbytery, the members simply "gave up" in discouragement and scattered, and have pretty generally identified themselves with other churches. The church lot has been sold to the Episcopalians, and the proceeds are held in trust for any future resuscitation of the congregation, or otherwise for the general interests of the United Presbyterian Church.

In February, 1858, the congregation of Big Spring gave a call to the Rev. Isaiah Faries, of the Presbytery of Caledonia, New York. This call was accepted, and during the summer he entered upon the discharge of his pastoral duties. His installation did not immediately take place, and during the next spring he made a visit to western New York, and from there sent back the call and asked for a certificate of dismission, without assigning any very satisfactory reason, and never returned. After a short time he removed to Minnesota, where he still lives, and preaches in the Presbyterian Church as his feeble health permits.

In August, 1859, a call was given to the Rev. John G. Brown, which was declined. In June of the following year another call was given to the Rev. W. L. McConnell, but from prudential and satisfactory reasons, it was not prosecuted before the Presbytery. In November of the same year, a call was given to William L. Wallace, which was accepted, and on the 13th of June, 1861, he was ordained and installed, and remained as pastor until May 15, 1879, when he resigned.

During the summer of 1859 this congregation erected a brick parsonage forty feet square and two stories high; and in the autumn and winter of 1868 a new brick church, eighty-two by fifty-five feet on the ground and two stories high, on the site of the old building. These two improvements cost in the aggregate nearly, if not altogether, twenty thousand dollars, and as this congregation has always regarded a church debt as a moral as well as a pecuniary encumbrance, in this case as in all previous ones, they paid as they went. On the first of January, 1874, they abolished all subscriptions and pew rents, and began to raise all moneys for salary, current expenses and the Boards of the Church, by weekly contributions on the " envelope system," and thus far the system has worked well.

The union of 1858 was soon followed by new combinations of the pastorates in York county. In June, 1859, Mr. McBurney was released from the branch of his charge in Lower Chanceford, and it was united with the old Associate Reformed congregation of that township into a pastorate, and on the 10th of August he was installed as pastor of the Hopewell congregation for one-third of his time. On the 6th of October, 1868, Mr. McBurney resigned the charge of Guinston and Hopewell, and on the 25th of April, 1871, the Rev. Samuel Jamison was installed as his successor. On the 28th of June, 1875, he was released from the Hopewell branch, since which time he has confined his labors entirely to the Guinston congregation. Hopewell was now united by Presbytery to the church in Gettysburg, and on the 12th of October, 1875, the Rev. John Jamison was installed as pastor for one-half of his time.

On the 23d of October, 1861, T. F. Baird was ordained and installed as the first pastor of the consolidated congregation in Lower Chanceford; but his health did not long permit him to hold the position, so, on the 26th of April, 1865, he resigned, but, on the 14th of June, before the Presbytery had time to act upon it, he died, and thus passed away, young in years but ripe in grace. On the 11th of September, 1866, they gave a call to their former pastor, Rev. W. Carlile, but he did not think that the state of his health would warrant his return. In September of the next year, they gave a call to the Rev. John Jamison, but he did not accept; and the next year they called D. G. Bruce, who accepted, and was ordained and installed on the 18th of May, 1869. He resigned, June 22d, 1872, and moved to the west. On the 29th of April, 1875, A. S. Aiken was ordained and installed, and is still in charge of Lower Chanceford.

After the departure of Mr. Simpson all connection between Carlisle and Unity, or Petersburg, ceased, and in June, 1857, the latter gave a call to the Rev. Joseph McKee, of the Associate Presbytery of Philadelphia, then teaching in Bloomfield, for part of his time. This call he accepted, and, on the 15th of July, he took charge of the congregation although he was never installed. He gave one-third of his time and divided it equally between the village of Petersburg and the northern wing at Milford or Middle Ridge. This arrangement continued till November, 1862, when he ceased to preach at Milford, but continued to supply at Petersburg till April, 1864, when he left the bounds of Presbytery. Petersburg, or Duncannon as now called, was joined by Presbytery to Gettysburg, to form a pastoral charge, and, on the 14th of April, 1868, the Rev. John Jamison was installed as pastor of these congregations. On the 1st of July, 1874, Mr. Jamison resigned Duncannon for the purpose of taking charge of Hopewell, in York county, since which time the former place has remained vacant, and has run down considerably in numbers and in prospects.

Shortly after the installation of Mr. Shields in Fermanagh, a trouble came which left for many years some unpleasant feeling. The old log church which had served the congregation from the period of its organization, had become quite uncomfortable, and a new house was a pressing necessity. A part of the congregation wished to build in the village of Mexico, which had sprung up not very far off, both for its geographical position, and for its town privileges and advantages.; while a respectable minority contended for the old site. The new church was built in the town, in 1837, and at the same time the congregation was incorporated, and its name changed to Mexico. During the incumbency of both Mr. Smith and Mr. Shields, one-third of the preaching to this congregation was done at Thompsontown.

Mr. Shields was never of robust frame or vigorous health, and during the last few years of his ministry was able to preach but once each Sabbath. In the spring of 1862, he was taken with a severe cold from which he did not entirely recover, and about the first of August he left for Minnesota, hoping to gain some benefit from its pure and bracing air. But on the journey he grew more feeble, so that when he arrived at Prairie du Chien, in Wisconsin, he was compelled to stop, and there, after a fortnight of severe illness, he died on the 19th of August, and his remains were brought home and interred among the dead of his flock in the old Fermanagh grave yard.

Mr. Shields was born in Pittsburgh, on the 11th of December, 1812, and was educated at the Western University of his native city, and at the Theological Seminary in Allegheny, and was ordained and installed on the 18th of June, 1835, in Fermanagh, where he remained till his death. He was rather small in stature, and fragile in body, with a good face and an expressive eye, and possessed a strong clear voice which he used very effectively in reading the Scriptures, and particularly in reading the Psalms. He was not gifted with fluency of utterance, so that in conversation as well as in the pulpit, he was of slow and hesitating speech. He had a good mind, clear and logical, was fond of good books and cultured companions, and had made good use of both, so that as a writer, he was very decidedly above the average minister, both in style and in matter. In private he was very cheerful, companionable, and witty, but his great modesty and diffidence prevented him from taking any prominent part in public meetings. Barring his slowness of speech, to which his people soon became accustomed, his pulpit performances were good, and sometimes decidedly excellent; while in his guileless simple-heartedness, cheerful hospitality, and consistent life, he might with much propriety have said with Paul, "Be ye followers of me, even as I also am of Christ."

That Mexico might receive more than the half time of a pastor, the long connection between it and Tuscarora was dissolved on the 14th of May, 1863, and the small congregation of Reedsville was united with it in a pastoral charge. The Rev. Joseph McCartney took charge of Mexico, on the first Sabbath of November, 1862, as stated supply, and on the 18th of May, 1863, he received a call to the pastorate of it and Reedsville, which he accepted, although his installation did not take place until the 14th of the following April. Mr. McCartney resigned on the 10th of July, 1867, and passed from the Presbytery. On the 21st of October, of the following year, this charge gave a call to John C. McElree, which was declined. On the 28th of September, 1869, Presbytery separated Reedsville from

Mexico, and installed the Rev. Francis McBurney as pastor of the latter for full time, which relation still continues, and the congregation is gradually growing.

Reedsville was disjoined from Stone Valley in the autumn of 1858, and subsequently joined to Mexico, but the death of William Cummins, its last elder, on the 1st of April, 1865, disorganized the congregation, and as it had so run down that there were no suitable men for the office, it was put temporarily under the supervision of the session of Mexico. But time and culture brought no improvement, and in the autumn of 1869, it was separated from the charge, and on the 22d of April, 1873, when it had on its roll only *three* male and *seven* female members, the Presbytery formally disbanded it, and sold its property.

For several years before his death, Mr. Shields felt unable to perform the duties of his office to both his congregations, so with the consent of Presbytery, he made a private arrangement in 1857 or '8 with the Rev. Joseph McKee to take charge of the congregation of Tuscarora as stated supply, although he still retained the pastoral office. Mr. McKee continued thus till the 1st of April, 1864, when he left the Presbytery for the west.

Mr. Jones continued to supply the congregation of Concord till the 11th of April, 1860, when he left the bounds of the Presbytery. On the 10th of September, 1861, the Rev. Joseph McKee began to supply it for one-fourth of the time, in connection with Tuscarora and Duncannon; and when he left in the spring of 1864, it was united with Tuscarora in a pastoral charge. On the 20th of April, 1865, the Rev. John A. McGill was installed as pastor of Tuscarora and Concord, and his labors in both have been signally blessed in the conversion of sinners and in the strengthening of believers.

After the separation of Reedsville from Stone Valley in 1858, the latter gave a call to John M. Adair for all his time, which was accepted, and on the 16th of March, 1859, he was ordained and installed as pastor, and has so remained with comfort to himself and profit to his people. This was one of the last official acts of the Associate Presbytery of Philadelphia.

The Rev. James A. McKee was received as a member of the Presbytery on the 11th of April, 1860, but remained only a short time.

The Rev. Chauncey Webster was received on the 25th of April, 1871, and dismissed in October, 1874, and received back again on the 24th of April, 1877.

On the 16th of April, 1862, the Presbytery passed unanimously the following resolution in reference to the Civil War then in progress:

"*Resolved*, That as an ecclesiastical body, and as citizens of the United States of America, we hereby express our cordial and hearty approval of the efforts of our Government to suppress rebellion, and declare ourselves the true friends and supporters of the Government in her efforts to establish her authority over all the States of the Union."

When the war was ended, and President Lincoln had been assassinated, the Presbytery, on the 26th of April, 1865, took further action, and resolved,

"1st. That in the sore judgments of the war, we recognize the hand of God directing us to humble ourselves and to repent of our sins as individuals, as families, as a Church, and as a Nation.

"2d. That in the assassination of the President, occurring as it did, in the hour of national triumph, we recognize the hand of an Allwise but Mysterious Providence; also, the real spirit of the rebellion, a spirit defiant of all law, liberty, justice and right; also, the duty of the Government to deal more rigidly with all that talk, and write, and act assistingly of rebels.

"3d. That we raise our protest against the course of the Government in its lenient dealing with known leading rebels. The teaching of God's word, justice, and all regard for public safety, demand that they shall be punished by death.

"4th. That we give our heartiest support to the Government in its efforts towards "National Reform," as manifested in the emancipation proclamation of the President, his expressed determination in regard to slavery in the re-construction of the States, and the resolution of Congress to amend the Constitution so as to prohibit slavery, from the States and Territories forever.

"5th. That we will labor in all proper ways to obtain further amendment to the Constitution, recognizing our national subordination to Christ as the Prince of the Kings of the earth.

The use of "tokens" in connection with the dispensation of the Lord's Supper had become so entirely perverted from their

8

original design, and the state of society had so changed as to leave no occasion for their proper and appropriate use, that a desire to lay them aside was expressed in some places, and as the custom was too venerable to be disregarded without some ecclesiastical sanction, the Presbytery saw fit, on the 24th of April, 1867, to resolve, " That whereas the use of tokens in the administration of the Lord's Supper is not required by any law of the Church, but is only a traditional custom ; therefore any session which may deem it expedient may dispense with their use."

All questions of public or private morality which have been brought to the attention of this Presbytery, have found in it at all times and under all circumstances an earnest and an active laborer for the right. And as the Church for the last generation has been devising new enterprises, and has been putting forth greater exertions to advance the cause of Christ in the world, so has this Presbytery being animated with the same spirit and zeal, and has exerted itself to stimulate its congregations to greater earnestness of spirt and liberality in contributions.

The Presbytery is at present in as good condition for doing its appropriate work as at any former period. The congregations are at peace within their own borders and with each other ; they are all in possession of comfortable church buildings, and some of them of parsonages ; the pastors are all in the prime of manhood ; and prayer meetings and Sabbath schools are every where recognized and employed as important aids in the impartation of knowledge and in the culture of the graces of the Spirit.

The history of this Presbytery clearly illustrates two facts. First, that the prudent and industrious pastor, without any special intellectual gifts, meets with better success in his work, than his more brilliant but less prudent brother. And second, that the influence of the pulpit upon the pews is so strong, that it takes but a short time for a minister of fair ability and prudence, to press himself upon the minds and affections of his people, so that they will think in things ecclesiastical very much as he does, and follow to a large extent where he leads. As

long as he is faithful to the interests and enterprises of his denomination so will they, and when he defaults in reference to
these things he will never be without followers.

It is but a proper expression of gratitude to say in conclu-
sion, that "the Lord has done great things for us, whereof we
are glad." Difficulties have always surrounded our location
and our work, and peculiar dangers have sometimes sorely
pressed, yet the Great Shepherd, knowing "our works and
tribulation, and poverty," has preserved us in our place, and
sustained us in our work, and made us the instruments of
bringing many sons and daughters home to glory. "Great and
marvellous are Thy works, Lord God Almighty; just and true
are Thy ways, thou King of Saints."

The congregations under the care of this Presbytery have
supplied the Church with a large number of ministers, many of
whom have been distinguished for their learning, their piety,
and their usefulness. It is now impossible to give a complete
list of these, not only because the records of the successive
Presbyteries are defective, but because a great number of them
moved westward with the families to which they belonged,
before they had advanced far enough to need Presbyterial
supervision, and thus finished their education elsewhere, and
entered the ministery under other agencies. Still to all intents
and purposes they were the children of this Presbytery, for
their characters and purposes were largely moulded here.
Elijah Scroggs, thirty-three years pastor of the Associate
Church of West Beaver and connections; his nephew Joseph
Scroggs, D. D., fifty-seven years pastor of the Associate Church
of Fairfield, Westmoreland county; Abraham Anderson, D. D.,
long professor of theology in the Associate Seminary at Canonsburg; Joseph McElroy, D. D., the first Associate Reformed
pastor in Pittsburgh, and then for fifty years a useful pastor in
New York; Henry Connelly, a life-long laborer in the State of
New York; Robert and Randall Ross, well known in the west,
were all born and partly educated within the bounds of the
single congregation of Big Spring, but moved with their families to the west before they had become students of theology.
Other congregations may not be able to name as many of this

class as this, yet they all had doubtless some.   In addition to this, a large number of those who still retained their home and church membership within our bounds, were not licensed by this Presbytery, nor were they ever subject to it as students. This arose from the fact that they found it more convenient, for different reasons, to connect themselves with the Presbytery of Monogahela, or some other one near to the theological seminary where they were pursuing their studies.

The following is an imperfect list of those who were born within the congregations of this Presbytery, and educated for the ministery while claiming this as their home, although many of them were licensed elsewhere:

William Baldridge was born of Irish parents in North Carolina, in March, 1760, was graduated at Dickinson College, and studied theology with Alexander Dobbin of Gettysburg, was licensed by the Presbytery of Pennsylvania in 1791, and was ordained in August, 1793, by the same Presbytery as pastor of the congregations of the Forks of the James River, Rockbridge county, Virginia, where he remained as pastor till 1803, and as stated supply till 1809, when he took charge of Cherry Fork and West Fork congregations in Adams county, Ohio, where he died on the 26th of October, 1830.

William B. Barr of Huntingdon county, was educated at Westminster College and Allegheny City, and was licensed April 23d, 1878.

W. J. Brown, of Augusta county, Virginia, admitted as student of theology April 28, 1847, and died in 1850.

George Buchanan was born in York county in 1782, was educated at Dickinson College, and in the Theological Seminary in New York, was licensed in December, 1809, and was ordained in Steubenville, Ohio, on the 4th of June, 1811, where he remained till his death, October 14, 1855.

Robert G. Campbell, of York county, was educated at Franklin College and Allegheny City, was licensed April, 1861, and ordained November 23, 1863, is now pastor of the United Presbyterian congregation of New Athens, Ohio, and professor in Franklin College.

William Carlile, of Shippensburg, was educated at Canonsburg and Allegheny City, was licensed April 18, 1843, and ordained to the pastorate of Lower Chanceford and Hopewell, October 25th, 1848, and is now without charge.

David Carson was born at Green Castle, in Franklin county, October 25th, 1799, was graduated at Canonsburg, studied theology two years under Dr. Mason until the Seminary was closed, and then finished with Dr. Banks, in Philadelphia, was licensed October 8th, 1823, and ordained in October of the following year as pastor of Big Spring and connections in East Tennessee; was elected professor of Hebrew and Church History in the Associate Seminary, in 1833, and died at Canonsburg on the 25th of September, 1834.

John X. Clarke was born in Franklin county, was educated at Dickinson College and the Theological Seminary in New York, was licensed September 12th, 1809, and ordained during the following year as pastor of the Second Associate Reformed congregation in New York city; he died comparatively young.

Thomas B. Clarkson was the son of the Rev. James Clarkson of York county, and was born in 1794, was graduated at Canonsburg, studied theology with Dr. Anderson, was licensed in 1820, ordained *sine titulo* in 1822, and installed as pastor of Mercersburg and the Cove October 8th, 1823, and died in 1836.

Abraham Craig was born in Ireland, and came to the Big Spring when his father assumed the charge of that congregation, was graduated at Dickinson College in 1795, was licensed by the First Presbytery of Pennsylvania, and ministered for over thirty years to congregations in Kentucky, Western Pennsylvania and Ohio.

Cyrus Cummins was born in Huntingdon county, graduated at Washington College, studied theology at Canonsburg, was ordained October 22d, 1846, as pastor of Ceasar's Creek, Ohio, and is now pastor of Mount Jackson, Pennsylvania.

James L. Dinwiddie, D. D., was born in Adams county, February 23d, 1798, was graduated at Washington College, studied theology under Dr. Mason, was ordained to the pastorate of the Mercer church on the 22d of November, 1820, was elected professor of theology in 1843, and died in January, 1849.

Robert G. Ferguson was born in the Concord congregation,

was educated at Canonsburg and Allegheny City, and ordained
and installed on the 17th of October, 1866, as pastor of Mercersburg and the Cove, and is now pastor of the church in
Butler.

S. G. Fitzgerald was born in Tuscarora, was graduated at
Westminster and studied theology in Allegheny, was licensed
on the 28th of April, 1872, and ordained May 4th, 1874, as
pastor of the Fifth church in Philadelphia, and is now pastor
of the Third church of the same city.

John Freetly was born in York county, was educated at the
Western University and Allegheny City, was licensed April
17, 1839, and has preached mainly in Illinois.

Matthew L. Fullerton was born in Green Castle, was graduated at Union College, commenced the study of theology under
Dr. Mason, and finished at Princeton, succeeded John Lind as
pastor of Hagerstown and Green Castle in 1825, and died in
1833.

Robert Gracey, D. D., was born near Newville, in 1811, was
educated at Canonsburg and Allegheny City, was ordained
August 3, 1837, was pastor of Chambersburg, Concord, Gettysburg, and Fourth church, Pittsburgh, and died July 10th, 1871.

J. L. Grove was born in York county, was educated at
Westminster and Allegheny City, was licensed, April, 25th,
1871, and ordained as pastor of Worthington, October 23d, 1872.

John E. Heannon was born near Newville, was educated at
Canonsburg and Allegheny City, was licensed April 25th, 1832,
ordained November 13th, 1833, preached in Kentucky, Indiana
and Oregon, died June 17th, 1863.

J. C. Hunter, of Huntingdon county, was graduated at Westminster College, studied theology at Allegheny City, and was
licensed May 7, 1879.

Samuel Irvine, D. D., was born in Huntingdon county, was
graduated at Canonsburg and studied theology with Dr. Anderson and was for many years pastor of the Associate congregation of Salt Creek, Ohio, and died a few years ago.

James Johnson, D. D., was born in York county in 1788, was
educated at Washington College and New York Theological

Seminary, was licensed June 27th, 1821, ordained May 2d, 1822, as pastor of Mansfield, Ohio, and died March 12th, 1858.

Jeremiah R. Johnson, D. D., was born in Franklin county, was educated at Westminster and Allegheny City, was licensed April 10, 1861, and ordained June 18, 1863, to the pastorate of Washington, Pennsylvania.

Matthew B. Johnson was born in York county, was educated at Canonsburg and Allegheny City, and died in 1836, on the eve of licensure.

Thomas Johnston was born in the Cove in Fulton county, was educated under the presbyterial direction of Messrs. Mc-Naughton and Webster, and is pastor of the Presbyterian Church of Talley Cavey, Pennsylvania.

Joseph Kerr, D. D., was born in Ireland, 1778, was graduated at Glasgow University, commenced the study of theology under Dr. Rodgers at Ballybay, came to the United States in 1801, settled temporarily near Newville, continued his studies under the First Presbytery, was licensed by the Monongahela Presbytery, April 27th, 1803, was ordained April 25th, 1804, was pastor of the congregations of St. Clair and Pittsburgh, was elected professor of theology in 1825, and died November 12th, 1829.

Joshua Kennedy was born in Franklin county, was educated under the auspices of the Reformed Presbyterian Church, (O. S.,) was ordained in the autumn of 1845, as pastor of the Conecocheague church, and is now pastor in Delaware county in New York.

R. W. Kidd was born in Tuscarora, was educated at Westminster and Newburg, N. Y., was licensed April 29, 1875, and was ordained as pastor of the Seventh Avenue church, New York, October 12th, 1876.

John Knox, D. D., was born in Adams county June 17th, 1790, was educated at Dickinson College and the New York Theological Seminary, was licensed in the spring of 1815; he and his seminary classmate Pascal N. Strong, D. D., were ordained July 14th, 1816, as pastors of the Collegiate Reformed Dutch Church in the city of New York, of which Drs. Kuypers and Milledoler were also pastors. He remained here in active labors till the 8th of January, 1858, when he died from a fall.

John M. Krebbs, D. D., was born in Hagerstown, Maryland, of German Reformed parentage; was reared and united with the church under the ministry of John Lind, was educated at Dickinson College and Princeton Seminary, and spent his life as pastor of one of the leading Presbyterian churches in New York city.

John Lind was born in Franklin county March 14th, 1784, was graduated at Dickinson College in 1802, studied theology for a season with his brother-in-law, Dr. Hemphill of South Carolina, then with Alexander Dobbin and John Young, and finished in the first class of the Seminary in New York, was licensed August 4th, 1807, was ordained October 4th, 1808, as pastor of Green Castle, Mercersburg, and the Cove, and died September 20th, 1824.

William H. Logan was born near Dillsburg, and is preaching in the Presbyterian Church of Millerstown, Pennsylvania.

James W. Logue was born in York county, was educated at Union College and Canonsburg Seminary, was licensed July 6, 1841, and ordained October 4, 1843, at Northfield, Ohio, where he still remains.

John R. McCallister was born in York county, educated at Franklin College and Allegheny City, was licensed in 1853, was ordained in October, 1855, exercised his ministry in western Illinois, and is now at Shippensburg, without a charge.

Joseph McCarroll, D. D., was born at Shippensburg July 9, 1795, was educated at Washington College and New York Theological Seminary, was licensed June 19, 1821, ordained as pastor of the church at Newburg, New York, March 14, 1823, which he retained till his death, March 29, 1864, he was also elected professor of theology in 1829, and discharged the duties thereof for thirty years.

George McCormick was born and reared within the Concord congregation, was educated at Amherst, Massachusetts, and Allegheny City, was ordained to the pastorate of Butler, October 22, 1872, and is now pastor of the congregation at Salinas, California.

James McCulloch, (son of James,) born at Big Spring, studied medicine, then went into the ministry of the Presbyterian Church, and died at Muncie, Indiana, in May, 1877.

John Scouller McCulloch, born at the Big Spring, educated at Canonsburg and Allegheny City, was licensed April 9, 1857, ordained pastor of the church in Peoria, Illinois, August 23, 1859, served as chaplain in the rebellion, then pastor of a Church in New York city, and now President of Knoxville College, Tennessee.

John W. McCullough, D. D., (son of John,) born near Newville in 1800, was graduated at Dickinson College in 1825, was ordained in the Presbyterian Church, and soon afterwards took orders in the Episcopal Church, and officiated many years in Wilmington, Delaware, and died October 14, 1867.

Samuel J. McCullough, (brother of J. W.,) born near Newville in 1810, was graduated in Dickinson College in 1829, was pastor of the Presbyterian Church in Tioga, Pennsylvania, for many years, and died December 19, 1867.

William McCullough, (son of William,) was born near Newville, entered Dickinson College in 1830, studied law and practiced it for many years, was then ordained an elder in the Baptist Church, and is now located in Texas.

John A. McGill was born in Huntingdon county, was educated at Franklin College and Canonsburg, was licensed in October, 1850, and ordained October 7, 1851, as pastor of Beaver congregation, and after occupying several other positions, is now pastor of Tuscarora and Concord.

William J. McGill was born in Huntingdon county, was educated at Union College and Canonsburg Seminary, was licensed in October, 1852, and after preaching two years, died on the 19th of March, 1855.

John McJimsey, D. D., was born near Gettysburg August 18, 1872, was graduated at Dickinson College, studied theology under his pastor, Alexander Dobbin, and also John Smith, of Octorara, was licensed in May, 1794, was ordained, *sine titulo*, on the 24th of September, 1795, was on the 22d of December, 1796, installed as pastor of Neelytown and Graham's Church, Orange county, New York, in 1809 went to Albany, and in

1815 to Poughkeepsie as a teacher, returned in 1819 to Graham's Church, and died as its pastor August 26, 1854.

Matthew McKinstry was born in Juniata county, (Mexico,) was educated at Western University and Allegheny City, was licensed April 14, 1835, ordained and installed over Bethesda and Laurel Hill April 27, 1836, and died December 10, 1872.

Gilbert McMasters, D. D., was born near Belfast, Ireland, on the 13th of February, 1778, in 1791 his father's family moved to this country and settled in Franklin county, he was educated at Canonsburg, first studied medicine and practiced two years in Mercer, was licensed in October, 1807, and was, on the 8th of August, 1808, ordained and installed over the Reformed Presbyterian Church of Duanesburg, New York, and in 1840 removed to Princeton, Indiana, and died March 17, 1854.

Joseph S. Maughlin was born in York county, was educated at Franklin College and Canonsburg Seminary, was licensed in October, 1851, and was ordained on the 21st of October, 1852, labored for some years in southern Indiana, and is without charge at Onawa, Iowa.

Thomas V. Moore, D. D., was born in Newville in 1818, was graduated at Dickinson College, studied theology at Princeton, was ordained in 1842, was pastor of Presbyterian churches in Carlisle, Green Castle, Richmond, Virginia, and Nashville, Tenn., in this latter place he died in 1871.

John Augustine Moore, (brother of T. V.,) was born in Newville in 1830, was educated at Princeton College and Seminary, was pastor of the Presbyterian congregation of Cub Creek, Virginia, and died in 1863.

———— Peoples was born in the Cove, in Fulton county, was educated under the auspices of Messrs. McNaughton and Webster, and is preaching in the Reformed Presbyterian Church at Northwood, Ohio.

Elder Piper, was born near Big Spring, was educated at Dickinson College and the Seminary in New York, and died upon the threshhold of the ministry in 1820.

Francis Pringle, jr., was born in Ireland, about 1789, came with his father to Carlisle in 1802, was educated at Dickinson College and under Dr. Anderson, was ordained and settled over the Associate congregations of Xenia and Sugar Creek, Ohio, in November, 1811, and died March 15, 1818.

James Pringle, (another son of Francis Pringle, Sr.,) was born in Ireland about 1788, was educated at Dickinson College and under Dr. Anderson, was ordained in April, 1814, and installed over the congregation of Steel Creek, North Carolina, and died October 28, 1818.

David Proudfit was born in York county, in 1771, studied theology under John Jamieson, was licensed April 5, 1795, ordained and installed November 14, 1798, over Laurel Hill, and connections, in Fayette county, moved to Crooked Creek, Ohio, April, 1824, and died June 11, 1830.

Robert Proudfit, D. D., was born in York county about 1778, was graduated at Dickinson College in 1798, studied theology with his cousin, the Rev. Dr. Alexander Proudfit, was licensed April 21, 1802, was ordained pastor of the congregation of Broadalbin, New York, on the 10th of April, 1804, was transferred to the professorship of languages in Union College, Schenectady, New York, in October, 1818, where he remained more than forty years, having been pensioned by that institution after he became superannuated.

Samuel B. Reed, D. D., was born in Huntingdon county, was educated at Franklin College and Canonsburg Seminary, was licensed in 1856, was ordained pastor of the First Associate church in Pittsburgh, April 18, 1847, and is now at Knoxville, Tennessee.

John Y. Scouller, D. D., was born near Newville, was graduated at Canonsburg and Allegheny City, was licensed May 1, 1844, and ordained as pastor of the congregation of Fair Haven, Ohio, on July 21, 1847, where he still remains.

James B. Scouller was born near Newville, was graduated at Dickinson College and Allegheny Seminary, was licensed April 19, 1842, was ordained pastor of the Second Associate Reformed congregation of Philadelphia November 13, 1844, was subsequently pastor in Cuylerville and Argyle, New York, and is now infirm.

Alexander Sharp. D. D., was born near Newville June 12, 1796, was graduated at Canonsburg, studied theology under

Dr. Mason, and finished under Dr. Riddell, was licensed in the spring of 1823, was ordained September 8, 1824, and installed pastor of Big Spring and Chambersburg September 29, 1824, and died January 28, 1857.

William Smith was born in York county, was educated at Franklin College and Canonsburg Seminary, was licensed July 10, 1839, was ordained a pastor in Iowa, August 25, 1841, afterwards settled in Western Pennsylvania and in Wisconsin, and died July 16, 1873.

Samuel F. Smith was born on the ocean in 1799, was graduated at the Western University, finished his theological studies under Dr. Kerr, in Allegheny City, was licensed August 17, 1826, was shortly afterwards ordained pastor of Cochranton, Crawford county, where he died March 19, 1846.

John Steele was born in York county December 17, 1772, was graduated at Dickinson College in 1792, studied theology with John Young while at Timber Ridge, Va., was licensed May 25, 1797, and ordained, *sine titulo*, on the 12th of August, 1799, was soon afterwards installed as pastor of Hinkston and connections in Kentucky, moved to Xenia, Ohio, in 1817, and died there on the 11th of January, 1837.

Robert Steel was born near Newville in 1813, was educated in Canonsburg and Princeton Seminary, was ordained as pastor of the Presbyterian church in Lewistown, Fulton county, Illinois, in 1844, and died there in 1848.

George Stewart was born at Green Castle in 1782, was graduated at Dickinson College, studied theology under Dr. Mason, was licensed in June, 1809, was ordained in April, 1810, as pastor of the congregation in Bloomingburg, New York, where he died September 20, 1818.

John G. Smart, D. D., was born in Huntingdon about 1804, graduated at Canonsburg, and studied theology under Dr. Banks, was licensed in 1827 or '8, was pastor of the Associate congregation in Baltimore for a number of years, and died in the summer of 1862, without charge.

James P. Smart (a younger brother of J. G.) was born in Huntingdon, graduated and studied theology at Canonsburg, was licensed in 1837, and was many years pastor of the Associate congregation of Massie's Creek, Ohio, where he died in 1861.

Robert B. Taggart was not a native of this region, but resided within its bounds while a student of theology, and studied under the Presbytery's supervision, was ordained, September 2d, 1869, as pastor of North Kortright, New York, and is now pastor at Mt. Pleasant, Pennsylvania.

T. J. C. Webster was born near Mercersburg, studied theology at Xenia, was licensed in 1877, and was ordained and installed as pastor of Santa Ana, California, in April, 1879.

Isaac A. Wilson was born in Concord, was educated at Franklin College and Allegheny City, was licensed in 1862, was ordained July 5th, 1866, by the Mansfield Presbytery, and is now at Pana, Illinois.

James Wallace was born in York county, studied theology at Canonsburg, was ordained by the Associate Presbytery of Miami, October 25th 1832, and died November 30th, 1878.

James S. Woodburn was born near Newville, educated at Canonsburg and Allegheny City, was licensed April 8, 1861, was ordained pastor in Gettysburg, May 10, 1864, and is now in the Presbyterian Church without charge.

John Young was born in York county September 4, 1768, was graduated at Dickinson College, studied theology under Dr. Nisbet of Carlisle, was licensed on the 26th of April, 1790, was ordained pastor of Timber Ridge and Old Providence, Virginia, August 20th, 1792, removed in 1799 to Green Castle, where he died July 24th, 1803.

John C. Young, D. D., (son of John,) was born in Green Castle August 12th, 1803, was educated at Dickinson College and Princeton Seminary, was licensed in the spring of 1827, was ordained in 1828, as pastor of the McCord Church in Lexington, Kentucky, and in 1830, was elected President of Centre College, which position he held till his death on the 23d of June, 1857.

Robert G. Young was born near Gettysburg, was educated at the Western University and Allegheny City, was licensed June 29th, 1869, was ordained to the pastorate of Butler, September 5th, 1871, and is now without charge.

When this history was passing through the press, a late pub-
lication of the Dauphin County Historical Society fell into the
hands of the writer, by which he is enabled to locate the place
and to give the final history of the meeting house in which
Matthew Lind preached in Paxton, or Paxtang, as the Society
has decided to be the correct spelling. "It is in Lower Paxtang township, six miles east of Harrisburg, two miles north
of Paxtang church, on the road from Harrisburg to Horners-
town and Union Deposit." "On the 11th of September, 1795,
James Byers and James Wilson, executors of William Brown,
Esq., deceased, (Mr. Lind's oldest Elder), of Paxtang, offered
for sale a LOG HOUSE near the residence (of Mr. Brown) formerly
occupied as a house of worship by the Rev. Matthew Lind."
It was owned in 1877 by the family of Jacob Grove. This LOG
HOUSE "was used, within the memory of many persons yet living,
as a sheep-pen. It stood north of the grave yard, but close to
it. It has disappeared."

www.ingramcontent.com/pod-product-compliance
Lightning Source LLC
Chambersburg PA
CBHW032015010726
47493CB00007B/2406